About the Author

The author is a Director of his law firm in the City of London. Father to Lauren and Abbey, he shares his time with his partner Denise between their homes in London and Norwich.

I said I was making you something
And it would lead to me sinking to one knee
Now that this book is ready to read
I wonder…
Will you marry me?
XX

Dedication

With my immeasurable thanks to Tarina and her limitless patience.
With my love to my daughters Lauren and Abbey. I am so proud of you both. You are amazing people.
And my love to the most amazing girl, my partner Denise. The real Scarlet Kiss and without whom these stories would not exist.

Kevin Mitchell

THE DYING WISH OF PRIVATE JAMES THOMPSON
AND OTHER SHORT EROTIC TALES

AUSTIN MACAULEY
PUBLISHERS LTD.

A CIP catalogue record for this title is available from the British Library.

ISBN 9781786125996 (Paperback)
ISBN 9781786126009 (Hardback)
ISBN 9781786126016 (E-Book)
www.austinmacauley.com

First Published (2016)
Austin Macauley Publishers Ltd.
25 Canada Square
Canary Wharf
London
E14 5LQ

Contents

The Dying Wish of Private James Thompson

The firefight had been short but brutal and bloody.

The gun smoke hung low over the battlefield, the acrid smell enough to make eyes water and lungs cough.

The surviving soldiers now so numb to death, so used to senseless violence, so programmed to the loss of colleagues that name tags are removed from those lost with barely a second thought.

Knowing that the letters home to their desperate and heart-broken loved ones will tell of their bravery and fulfilled duty to their country.

Today the English had won, tomorrow it might be the turn of the Germans. This was France in 1917 and the war was at an impasse. Skirmish followed skirmish, neither side gaining any significant ground, neither side making that vital breakthrough.

The soldiers now sitting in small clusters, smoking the cigarettes they had looted from the pockets of their dead enemy, knowing tomorrow the Hun could so easily be smoking theirs.

Taking in what had once been beautiful countryside but was now little more than a half demolished village surrounded by deep shell holes half filled with muddy brown water.

The door of what had been the village Inn opens and Scarlet, armed with two bottles of the local homemade brandy, steps forward.

Not for the first time in this war, she is urged by others in her native tongue not to be so foolish, to sit tight in her home till the soldiers move on but she ignores them.

Her act is not partisan, nor one of collusion or conspiracy. Her act is one of compassion. Compassion for those fighting, those dying, those dead. Compassion for those they leave behind and who mourn their passing.

She walks towards who to her seems the most senior of the soldiers. She smiles and holds out her hand in greeting.

He bows slightly, removes his helmet and gently shakes her hand.

She has found similarities in all of the soldiers she has met from both sides. All a long way from home, most desperate to return. All have treated her with courtesy and respect. These soldiers are no different.

The small troop, no more than a dozen left, gather around her and accept her gift of the throat burning brandy. For many their first alcohol in weeks.

They try to share pleasantries but bar the Captain who has a smattering of her tongue; their languages are alien to each other.

Gradually the brandy calms the adrenalin that has rushed through the soldiers' bodies. The local villagers now emerge, satisfied of their safety. The soldiers start to swap cigarettes for bread and cheese.

Suddenly a cry,

"Captain, it's Thompson, I think he is still alive."

The Captain rushes to the scene, with Scarlet and two other soldiers not far behind.

The poor wretch lies staring out at those around him but for all other intents and purposes he is in a world of his own.

"Injuries?" asks the Captain

"None so far as I can see, sir."

The Captain has seen the signs before and crosses his chest in prayer. The shell has destroyed the poor man's mind and cracked his skull. The poor boy has but hours to live.

The Captain turns to Scarlet,

"Le garçon est en train de mourir, Pouvez-vous l'aider?"

(The boy is dying. Can you help him?)

In a flurry of French and animated energetic hand signals, Scarlet directs the soldiers to make a temporary stretcher, and once made, to slowly and steadily carry the injured soldier to her house.

The injured soldier sees Scarlet and frantically reaches for her hand, trying to reach and kiss it.

"Rosa, Rosa," he murmurs to her.

"Steady, lad," the Captain's voice urges restraint.

"My wife Rosa, my beautiful wife."

"Il pense que vous êtes sa femme."

(He thinks you are his wife, the Captain explains.)

"Le pauvre garçon," she brushes the soldier's fringe away from his eyes and softly urges "Là, calme-toi et sois tranquille."

(The poor boy. There, there, be calm and rest).

Much of the old Inn is uninhabitable. Beams, tiles and bricks have all imploded into various of the rooms and it takes barely a glimpse skywards to see the joists skeletal like holding what is left together.

Scarlet is greeted at the door by her husband, Pierre. The angry exchange is followed in part by the Captain who struggles with the speed of the exchange and the husband's accent.

The cause is clear. He does not want the soldier under their roof. This is not their war. They must not take sides.

Scarlet bristles and her response seethes with fire. She will care for him under their roof until he dies. Their body language is clear. Like fighting cocks, Scarlet is primed, Pierre as displayed in his slumped shoulders, is resigned to defeat.

The Captain offers his hand to Pierre. Pierre returns the gesture, with a hint of reluctance.

The wounded soldier is slowly lifted through the gaps in the stairs to Scarlet and Pierre's bedroom – one of the few rooms left fully intact.

The fire roars and the small lanterns and candles create an intimate glow. Scarlet and the Captain talk quietly in one corner out of ear shot from the wounded man.

The wound is such that he will fade slowly through the evening. If God is on his side, he will sleep soundly by night and never wake.

The wounded soldier calls

"Rosa, Rosa, where are you?"

Scarlet instinctively rushes to his side knowing that just being there will bring him comfort.

He taps on his breast pocket. One, two, three, four times. Scarlet unbuttons the pocket and pulls out the small locket. As she opens it a beautiful but melancholic tune fills the air but it is the picture inside that makes Scarlet stop, then stare, then gasp. It is her. The picture inside is of her.

She hands the locket to the Captain.

"Well I never…" he exclaims.

Pierre looks at the picture in the locket then at Scarlet, closes the locket, then shakes his head.

The soldier talks to her softly,

"Rosa, I know I do not have long. Maybe the night, please come lay with me. Like we used to. Bare as the day we were born."

The Captain translates. A dark cloud descends on Pierre's mood. He pours a deep glass of the rough brandy and drinks it in a single swallow.

Scarlet is filled with a wave of empathy and despite his genuine and heart felt concerns, assures the Captain she will be fine. She will sit with him through the night till he sleeps.

There is another angry exchange of words with Pierre after the Captain has left.

Pierre cannot shake off the coincidence in Scarlet and Rosa's appearance and has that developing sense of dread and nausea that only Scarlet knows just what she will do next.

Scarlet needs to think, think about the coincidence. To think how Rosa would feel if their positions were reversed.

The soldier soon eases into a sleep and Scarlet bathes his face with clean warm water. The Captain now fed and sure his men are settled joins the three and shares a glass of brandy with Pierre, placating him with cigarettes, jam and chocolate.

The next hour is spent in pleasant conversation, such as it can be. With a mix of French, English and actions, they initially discuss the terrible war, then nicer times, before the war and finally the coincidence of Scarlet and Rosa's appearance.

It is as that very subject is raised that the soldier calls again.

"Rosa, Rosa where are you?"

In her adopted role, Scarlet moves to his side.

"You are still so beautiful my darling," he smiles at her.

The Captain translates to the room. The soldier's fingers trace a path through Scarlet's hair, the beautiful features of her face, her chin, her neck. He pauses slightly then lets his fingers fall to the mounds of her firm, full breasts.

Pierre and the Captain both draw back their chairs to rise and restrain him, but Scarlet, without moving her torso puts out her hand to stop them.

"Je ne suis pas offensée. Il pense que je suis sa femme. Je ne vais pas le rier une intimate finale avec elle." (I am not offended. He thinks I am his wife. I will not deny him a final intimacy with her).

The soldier kneads Scarlet's breasts and rises just a little to seek out her mouth. She reaches down and lets his tongue slide softly between her lips.

The Captain starts to look away but turns back. The perversity overwhelmed by Scarlet's compassion.

Pierre's senses too are overwhelmed. The bile and anger rises through him like a volcano but there is just that twitch, that niggle. The anger aimed slightly at himself. Because he knows, but hates to admit, that somewhere deep is a seed of arousal as he watches his wife slowly being touched and now kissed by another man.

The kiss breaks, and the soldier regains his breath.

"Rosa you still kiss so beautifully. Is it so dreadful that even now, on this my death bed, all I want is you, all I can think of is you, your lips on me, your hands on me."

The Captain makes his apologies.

"I am sorry, monsieur, I will have him removed immediately."

"No I am afraid you cannot do that Captain; she will not let you. She would not let me let you. My wife believes she is doing the right thing. It does not matter what you or I think of her."

Scarlet heads to the Captain.

"Please do not worry Captain. You have had a very difficult day. You need rest. Pierre and I will care for your soldier. Your place is with your men."

For the first time Scarlet looks into the Captain's eyes and his weary now battle-hardened features. Probably only twenty-five he looks nearer forty. Already lined and greying at the sides. The light already turned out behind his eyes. His world a constant battle just to stay alive. He smiles a weary enigmatic smile of thanks. Pierre pulls a small floorboard to one side and reaches in pulling out another bottle of brandy.

"It's crap I know but it may help you and your men sleep just a little."

The Captain takes the bottle and nods to Pierre and holds his hand briefly as an acknowledgement of his heartfelt thanks, then leaves.

Pierre slumps back in his chair and throws a shot of the brandy pausing as the liquid fire burns its way to his stomach. He looks at Scarlet broodily.

"You cannot ask this of me," he growls.

"I can and I do," she retorts quietly but defiantly "The poor boy is a long way from home. He is dying. He thinks I am his wife. What if things were reversed? What if you were me?"

"I would remember I was your wife."

"Then Pierre you are not the man I thought you were. You used to be different to them all."

Pierre pours and sinks another shot

"I know I ask a lot of you but picture me not as me but as his wife. Stay and watch his wife pleasure him."

"We both know you will do what you want to do," was the gruff reply.

Gruff yes, but amounting in its resignation to the permission which Scarlet seeks.

"Rosa. Rosa" the soldier awake once again calls for his wife.

Scarlet looks to Pierre.

"Go," he says.

Thompson smiles as his beautiful Rosa appears once more before him. So beautiful with her piercing sapphire blue eyes and soft pouting mouth like a magnet to his.

"I am so sorry I am dying, my love. I know I promised I would come home safely but this darn war has cheated us both."

Scarlet knows nothing of what he says but realises he does so with love and sadness. She strokes his fringe away from his eyes and smiles at him. Waiting for his hands to wander across her once more. And they do. Slowly along her neck and shoulders, then down to the firm mounds of her breasts. He fumbles with the buttons of her blouse but lacks the coordination to undo more than one. With her eyes locked with Pierre's, Scarlet slowly unbuttons her blouse and lets it slide from her shoulders to the floor. Thompson's eyes shine as his hands gently cup then knead the mounds before softly stroking then pinching the soft pink nipples.

Thompson gently pulls Scarlet to him and folds his soft wet mouth around her nipples in turn. Sucking hard before letting his tongue flick just the very tip. With the tingles of pleasure washing through her, Scarlet instinctively presses her palm against the bulge growing in Thompson's trousers. Feeling under her hand the full length of his hard long shaft, feeling his gasp vibrate against her breast as she slides her palm up and down the full length.

Her hands unclip his fly buttons and reluctantly Thompson releases his mouth from her. Scarlet slides his trousers to his knees and takes in the outline of his long cock pressing against the restraint of his pants. Slowly she slides the pants down exposing him inch by long inch.

It takes both of her small hands to grip his full shaft. One at the base and one just below his foreskin. Sliding the foreskin over his glistening helmet, Scarlet slowly starts to pump him. Stretching the skin till it would seem that the sensitive filament will snap or tear.

And so this macabre but beautiful ménage a trois unfolds. For Thompson, knowing death nears, he has for one last time the hands of his beautiful wife Rosa intimately upon him. For the proud, besotted Pierre, he cannot now conceal the perverse pleasure he gains from watching his wife with this man. And for Scarlet, knowing the good she does for Thompson is now matched and will shortly be consumed by her own pleasure, fuelled by the eyes of Pierre upon her. Knowing that the more intimate she becomes, the more aroused he is. Knowing that when they are next together he will fuck her with an intensity they have never before known together.

It is this final thought that rolls through Scarlett's mind as with a soft smile and a final look into Pierre's eyes she lowers her mouth onto Thompson's cock.

Letting her tongue roll around the underside of the helmet before her small mouth has to stretch to take in its girth, hearing both Thompson and Pierre audibly gasp as the outline of the shaft fills and distorts her cheeks.

Her saliva starts to leak along the mighty shaft as slowly and inch by inch her mouth works its way along its length. Even when relaxing her gag reflex Scarlet cannot take it fully in. She looks across to Pierre. His mouth slightly open, brandy untouched in one hand, his other slowly rubbing the buttons of his fly against his own erect shaft.

"Fuck me, Rosa," Thompson groans through his own arousal. "Fuck me, my love."

Scarlet walks till she is in full view of Pierre and slides her trousers along her long toned legs till they crumple to the floor. She watches him so intently as her fingers in each side of her knickers tease them over her deliciously wide hips. Now entirely bare, Pierre can see her own arousal. Her pupils now melted and enlarged, her nipples hard and stretched, the tops of her thighs now glistening with the love juices leaking from her.

She turns ensuring Pierre's eyes are taking every moment of her in, and straddles Thompson's thighs.

Her body tenses and she lets out her own long slow groan as she first rubs that mighty purple helmet along her slit to her clit, then tries to force him into her. Even with the lubrication of her love juice she fears he is too big. But slowly her entrance stretches and folds itself around him letting him in. Rising and falling on him, she gradually takes the full length. Never has she been filled so completely, so fully. Her hands massage Thompson's chest seeing in his eyes not only his pleasure but the deep love he has for his wife, now once again consummated in this lovemaking. She turns to take in Pierre. That broody stare belies his arousal. She knows that well. His hands undo his fly and as Scarlet watches, his hand slips around his own shaft. Scarlet growls her pleasure as Thompson starts to roll his hips and fuck her ever deeper. Her body releasing ever more lubrication as she sees Pierre's fist slowly pumping himself up and down.

Now becoming lost in her own pleasure she starts to ride Thompson, together building that slow intense rhythm. His mighty cock pounding, abusing, teasing her G spot. She cannot control or delay her climax. The waves start from the tip of her little toe and make her entire being tremble. Her body jerks with the pleasure, tensing and relaxing in spasms. But he does not stop. Nor does he climax. The fire burning through her. Pierre's hand is starting to pump more fiercely in his pants.

The pleasure is now overwhelming and Scarlet slides herself from her impaling.

With hands invigorated with renewed strength Thompson turns the breathless Scarlet till her anus is now pressed against his helmet.

"No. No my love, you are too big," Scarlet warns.

Not understanding again Thompson tries gingerly to enter her.

"Pierre I need your help –"

Pierre stands now at the feet of Thompson seeing the huge cock trying to enter his wife's tiny anus. He has never before felt this sensation run through him. A mixture of shame, humiliation, disgust but also the purest deep arousal.

"What do you want me to do?"

"You need to lubricate me my love. You have to make it possible for me to take this."

"No. Enough!" he growls and starts to leave.

"You want me to rip then, rip and bleed? I will take this with or without you Pierre."

Pierre dithers but his mind is made up as he sees Scarlet try to lower her anus onto the mighty purple helmet.

"Stop. Spin around," he barks.

Scarlet spins offering her bare cheeks to Pierre and gently lowers her mouth to Thompson's cock, she kisses it once then slowly glides her soft, wet mouth just over his helmet with sufficient pressure not to bring him to climax but to retain his arousal.

She feels Pierre's firm fingers part her pale toned cheeks and his tongue glide over and around her puckered hole. The tingling nerve endings sending mini shocks of pleasure throughout her body. The tongue slowly lapping harder and harder, the tip gradually breaking through the resistance of her muscles.

Scarlet growls with Thompson's helmet deep within her mouth.

Then Pierre stops and walks to his bedside cabinet. He pulls the bottle of oil he thought would only ever be used by Scarlet and he.

Pouring the oil into the crack at the top of her cheeks he uses the pads of his fingers to work it into the surface of the small black puckered hole. Slowly, the muscles let a fingertip through, then a second.

Pierre's sensibilities are numb. His brain cannot rationally accept that he is preparing his beautiful wife's anus, one she so rarely lets him, her husband, use, for a stranger.

His lubricated fingers gradually ease their full length into Scarlet. His own cock aches and throbs as he can smell his wife's sex glistening on her slowly spasming pussy. The pussy he can see that has been stretched and used like it has never before, certainly never by him.

"You are as ready as I can make you," he whispers.

Scarlet spins so she has her back to Thompson and her front to Pierre. Pierre turns to leave, the sight of his beautiful wife like this almost too much for him.

"No stay, Pierre, I need you to help me balance."

Pierre looks away, her request for help not one he can process.

"Pierre, stay. Watch. I can see the pleasure this brings you. Enjoy it with me."

Scarlet once again tries lowering her anus onto Thompson's cock. She nearly topples forward. Pierre reaches out instinctively with his left hand and catches her right hand holding her still. Her small smile of her appreciation is replaced by a look of fear, pain and anticipation as the helmet presses hard and

23

more forcefully against her. Breathing now like she is mid contraction, puffing out her cheeks so slowly she stretches and at last the monstrous helmet is inside her.

Thompson slowly lets his hips rise and fall, his shaft gradually filling Scarlet ever deeper.

"Touch me, Pierre, touch me." With his fingers still oiled he presses them firmly through her hood onto her hard protruding clit. Then with their eyes locked he massages her in tender gentle circles.

With their hands still held and their eyes locked, Pierre watches the pain in Scarlet's eyes turn first to a dull ache and then a throbbing pleasure, one heightened by his oiled fingers.

He slides his fingers to her hole and as Thompson withdraws his shaft to the tip of his helmet Pierre slides his fingers deep inside her.

Scarlet cries out once as the pleasure consumes her and then again but louder, almost akin to a wild tortured beast, as Thompson slides almost his entire length back inside her anus.

Pierre's cock twitches as he feels Thompson's cock fucking his adored wife through the thin membrane separating it from his fingers.

Scarlet is now mumbling incoherently. From her mouth spills filth like a foul spirit being exorcised from her, arousing Pierre ever more.

Pierre feels her climax before her long moan fills the room. Her muscles spasming and gripping his fingers, but then Thompson comes, too, Pierre feeling that twitch and jerk of the shaft and the deep release of this other man's come deep, deeper than he had ever been into his wife's bowels. The release of come pulsing like a heartbeat against his fingers.

It seems like forever before Scarlet's breathing returns to normal. She kisses Pierre deeply on his mouth, the sheen of sweat on her exhausted face making her taste salty, before he helps her lift herself from Thompson. She still aches and hurts, but in a deliciously used and pleasured way.

She smiles a look of love to Pierre then lays her head on Thompson's chest. Her body still bare, her arm wrapped tight around his waist.

"I love you, Rosa," whispers Thompson as he gently strokes his fingers through Scarlet's hair.

Pierre finds a spare blanket and lays it across them. He pokes the glowing embers of the fire before loading it with more logs to ensure Scarlet remains warm through the night.

He blows out each candle till the room is lit only by the now burning logs and then sits on guard at his table with only the brandy for company

Private James Thompson dies peacefully in his sleep at 8.45 a.m. with his beloved Rosa still lying bare next to him. He is buried amongst the last surviving lavender beds, the perfume forever reminding Scarlet and Pierre of the intimacy with him.

Rosa was not surprised when the uniformed liaison officer had knocked at the door to their flat. Three weeks had passed, the longest ever, since the last letter had been received from her beloved James.

Despite being one of ten calls he had to make that day, the Officer broke the news to her with kindness and compassion. The tears had flowed just as soon as he had left and several hours had passed before she had found the strength to open the Captain's letter.

The letter that had enclosed her locket, had told of his incredible bravery, of the kindness shown to him by the French in his final hours and of his final words.

"Rosa, I will love you in this life and the next."

The Glory Hole

A glory hole: "A glory hole is a hole in a wall or other partition often between public lavatory stalls for people to engage in sexual activity or observe the people in the next cubicle whilst one or both parties masturbate. The partition maintains anonymity."

It had been one of those days. No not one of those days, one of *those* days. A day where the autumn sunshine had bought out the brightest reds, browns and ambers in the last leaves still hanging like brave survivors from the trees. Where the squirrels still scamper for the last of their winter feed and every man and his dog decides on a post lunch walk in the park.

That included Harry and I. Harry had been keen to snooze on the sofa on the pretext of watching the important game on TV, but with a mixture of bullying and vague sexual promises I had lured him from his intended slumber.

Now buoyed by our bracing stroll, Harry was back to his mischievous self.

"I have todays little game," he beamed as he strode all too confidently from the little cottage style public toilet hidden from the world by the small copse of trees.

"Go on," I said with an exaggeratedly faked interest.

Harry pulled me almost conspiratorially to one side.

"There's a glory hole in the toilet," he chattered.

"And?"

"Let's hang around till dusk. That will give us an hour before it closes. I'll make sure it's all clear then you can go ready yourself and I'll come back in."

Now I know I might be a little strange but the taboo in it all just stirred a little twinge in my pants. The thought of sitting where men sat and sucked anonymous cocks in fear of arrest just worked for me. Okay it's not a stranger's cock – its Harry's but once it appears through the hole in the wall...

We had lingered in the coffee bar by the lake people watching. As the families left, the young couples and odd single men entered then disappeared like ghosts into the trees.

"Amazing these little nether worlds we never see," beamed Harry as he exited the toilet. "Okay it's all clear. You need to go into the middle cubicle. Get yourself comfortable. Imagine you're a man. It's the late 1960s. I'm a stranger okay? I'll give you a minute to settle then join you."

The first thing that strikes you about a man's public toilet is that smell. That weird mix of piss, stale air and floral bleach. The second is the graffiti. Graffiti of football teams carved by fans into toilet doors. Graffiti of spray can logos. Graffiti of names and numbers written into the walls of the cubicles of supposedly local rent boys.

I had just settled onto the seat and started to read the advert for Nick, one such local rent boy when the main door to the toilet slammed closed. I found it difficult to supress a giggle but as I heard the door of the next cubicle open then close and the zip pulled open, I found myself glued to the hole separating us.

The diffused light created an almost ethereal atmosphere as I heard Harry tapping his cock against the cubicle wall to make sure it was super stiff for my mouth.

Then it appeared, thick stiff and curved. That was when I could understand the magic of a glory hole. That moment when a stranger's cock just appeared hoping for a discreet wet mouth. No questions asked. No names. No emotions. No faces. No strings. With those thoughts rolling in my imagination my mouth closed around the purple swollen knob.

Slowly allowing my tongue to tease his come hole before letting it roll over the entire knob. I just loved the sound of the first groan as my mouth closed over the knob and worked its way down the full length of the shaft.

I could feel Harry trying to force more of himself through the hole, then gradually pump himself forward rhythmically to meet me.

Hearing his pelvic bones thrust against the wall, his belt clanging like a badly set chime of a clock.

I could feel my forehead slowly meeting the wall. Deeper and deeper into my mouth.

Then that moment, when the cock twitches, when Harry holds his breath and the hot salty come erupts into my throat.

I barely hear his panting over my own. Our breath slowing in time. Then I hear the zip, the cubicle door open and close, then the main door swing shut.

I count to 60, taking the time to view what I suspect will be my only trip to a men's public toilet with its own glorious hole, before I wipe my mouth then leave.

"Well?" I beam at Harry as he joins me outside.

"Well?" he says.

"How was it for you?" I smirk

"It wasn't, was it? After you went in some idiot went in before I could join you."

The realisation of what might have just happened hit me a split second before Harry.

"Oh…" was all I could think to say.

The Air Raid

Scarlet's heart raced as the siren screeched its warning of impending doom on London's streets.

Of course she knew the Wermacht would continue its torture of the capital again tonight.

She had followed their path and the dogfight that had ensued between the fighter planes trying to help or hinder their progress on the massive air chart she helped to manage in the War Office in Whitehall. But they had miscalculated the size of the force and the time for which they could be delayed by a crucial thirty minutes.

The first distant anti-aircraft guns fire into the air with a muffled and comforting boom. The bus stops as the conductor shouts his sadly now all too familiar message to those few passengers still aboard.

"Okay, ladies and gentlemen, we all know what this means. All off please and try to head to the nearest shelter. Oh and may God be with you all."

The passengers including Scarlet scurry from the bus. She had been on her way home from her night shift but here now barely halfway back in Whitechapel she is entirely lost. She tries to follow where the other passengers have fled but they disappear like tiny mice through skirting boards.

She starts a route along a side street looking anxiously for shelter, the blackouts in each of the very few houses not evacuated effectively achieving their purpose.

Now alone on the street she jumps as the explosion roars behind her, the bus on which she had been travelling now a blazing twisted wreck. The hot air, even from this distance, flushing her face.

Another explosion – a house possibly only two streets away. She briefly looks to the sky and watches as the search lights pick out the swarm of bombers dropping their death and destruction.

Then the whistle, the whistle of the bomb falling from the sky ready to fall somewhere close, somewhere too close.

She starts to run as fast as she can suck the air into her lungs. Runs as fast as the tight pencil skirt pulled as high as decency permits will allow her.

The third explosion sends Scarlet into a blind panic as the shrapnel of wood, metal and brick fall like deadly snow around her.

Looking over the lower walls of the back yards still haunted with the ghosts of children playing and washing drying, she searches desperately for a shelter. Any shelter.

Now in Sydney Street, almost entirely abandoned, she strikes lucky as the glow from a burning coal bunker causes a small piece of the shelters roof to glint.

Struggling to climb the yard wall and with the next bomb whistling its melancholy tune of death towards her she whips her skirt from her girdled and stockinged legs and scrambles over its height.

A race now between her and the bomb, she throws herself down the sandbagged stairs and through the submerged door just as the house next door erupts like a seething volcano.

The shelter is pitch black. Scarlet scrambles with her hands until she feels a wooden bench and there she sits, skirt still in hand, as the tears come, slowly at first, single tears causing dust stained rivers along her beautiful cheek bones. But then they flow more freely until she weeps uncontrollably.

It is only when the first match is struck that she realises she is not alone.

They are together. Both in army uniform. She a redhead with looks as close to a movie star as you could wish, he handsome, green eyes, dark hair.

Her view of them lasts as long as it takes the match to light her cigarette and have the life shaken out of it.

Looking around the shelter, Scarlet sees two more glowing pin pricks from the lit cigarettes. That is all she can see. All she can see until the second match is lit. Two more soldiers. Barely a glimpse before the match dies.

"They are rotten shots. Hopefully we'll live for another night," the red head breathes through the darkness.

As if she has provoked fate another bomb falls nearby shaking the shelter and bringing a shower of dust from the ceiling.

Scarlet hears the red head scramble towards her then feels her sit beside her. She smells like women did before the war. Of perfume and lipstick and honeyed breath even after she takes a last drag and lets the tiny butt fall to the floor.

Her tiny hand folds inside Scarlet's and squeezes it reassuringly as her head tilts and rests on Scarlet's shoulder.

And there they sit in silence for what is perhaps 15 minutes but seems like forever. Scarlet starts to feel tired, her eyes starting to flutter and close, her brain now used to the violence outside. The woman's hand has fallen free and innocently, Scarlet is sure it must be innocently, comes to rest on the inside of her thigh.

But then slowly and hesitantly, as if waiting to be stopped the fingers start to stroke her. Gently, reassuring but now occasionally drifting onto the soft bare thigh above her stocking.

It is only as those fingers drift even higher, stroking just the bare thigh up to the gusset of her knickers that Scarlet fully wakes to a conscious state and holds her breath.

Her heart starts to race. Her hand instinctively reacts holding tight and stilling the woman's fingers.

Scarlet gradually releases the pressure on Red's fingers but it is mere seconds before they again start to play. Gliding the full length of Scarlet's thigh to her knee then all the way back to the crotch of her now dampening knickers.

She senses Red turn in towards her and feels her soft wet mouth slowly kiss her bare neck. She should stop her but she doesn't. Another match is lit catching in that brief flare of light Red's lips now seducing Scarlet's ear and jaw and, Scarlet closing her eyes as the tingles start to run like little electric shocks through her body.

"Don't panic just relax," whispers Red, "Just go with it, it's this stupid war it makes us all do crazy things."

Scarlet lets Red's fingers slowly unbutton the buttons on her jacket and slide it from her shoulders.

Scarlet's mind is a maelstrom of conflicting thoughts, morals, desires, principles, but most of all lust. What Red has said is true and that is Scarlet's prevailing thought. People do crazy things in crazy times. Besides Scarlet doesn't know any of these people. The thought of the men hearing the two women getting it on together but not being able to see is a delicious turn on. The odd lit match creating an occasional but teasing visual theatre.

Red's soft fragrant lips nibble across Scarlet's face towards her mouth. Scarlet sighs as mentally she releases herself from the chains of self-doubt and kisses Red. Their tongues twirl like an Argentine tango. Red pulling Scarlet's hair back to force her tongue deeper into her mouth.

Then the hand pressed against the mound of her breast. Even through her blouse and vest her nipple hardens and presses into the palm.

It takes seconds before she realises that it cannot be Red's hand. Red's hands are in her hair and on her thigh.

The buttons of her blouse are being opened, she cannot see anything in this darkness. Her hand scrambles to grab the man's hands and holds them tight.

"No," she moans into Red's mouth.

The second pair of hands take over where the first were stopped. Scarlet powerless to stop her blouse being opened, releases the grip on the hands she is holding and tries to pull the opened sides back together. Leaving herself vulnerable to the four strong hands pulling the sides open against her and sliding the material from her shoulders.

"Please no," she murmurs. "Please."

Red's mouth throughout folds around Scarlet's tongue sucking on it like a soft limp tingling cock, drowning her protests.

Her resistance broken and now powerless to stop the removal of the blouse. The hands, four of them now sliding under her vest. Kneading her bare mounds and pinching her hard nipples. Her slow moan into Red's mouth betraying her inner slut. Her hands outside of her vest trying to slow those strong hands under it. Massaging, groping, that relentless force, so much stronger than her.

The pleasure mounts inside her. Her hair is gripped tight and her head turned. A man's tongue so hungry for her. Like a starving man offered food. His mouth the opposite to the feline culture of Red. His mouth forcing Scarlet's wider. To her shame she responds, not reluctantly, not gently, but with the same intensity as he. Their mouths fucking with intent.

The third soldier her head tells her it must be. His strong hands force her thighs open. Her thigh muscles half-heartedly resisting but no match for this fit, muscular man. His hands holding them wide enabling Red with enough space now to slide her hand under the silk knickers. Her long nails glide between her sopping wet hood and press firmly against her hard clit. The sustained pressure makes Scarlet break from her kiss.

Her long moan of pleasure fills the shelter.

The relentless assault continues. One of the men is standing before her. His uniformed clad crotch pressed close to her face, making the back of her head touch the shelter wall. If she turns to the right the soldier's tongue will fuck her mouth, to the left Red's cat like tongue and before her, the buttons being forcibly ripped open, a long hard cock.

Her head is jerked back forcing her mouth open. Her mouth instinctively folds around the swollen knob drinking in the salty pre come.

Her hands in defiance of her overwhelmed sexual desires, push either side of his hips to force him away.

Her resistance is futile. Gradually she instead uses those same hands to pull him onto her mouth. Her saliva lubricating his curved aching shaft.

The third soldier slides her knickers from her. There is no resistance from her. Her sensibilities truly abandoned, just now craving pleasure, climax, satisfaction.

His strong hands slide her hips and bottom forwards, forcing everyone to slightly readjust. His tongue so delicately rolling around her rim drinking in the love juice that flows so freely coating his stubbled chin. The tip of the tongue tentatively breaking through her resistance, slowly fucking her cunt. The tongue so beautifully complimenting Red's fingers rolling around her clit.

Red now slowly sucking on her neck drawing the skin to a pinch, kneading her breast in a firm grip. The soldier the other side biting deep into her shoulder as the tips of his fingers brush the tips of her nipples – so, so lightly.

Her cry starting so deep and rising like marble steps to that of an angel's. The waves roll like lava through her loins. Her brain flashing a series of pictures of her being used, violated and abused before like a firework display, the colours fire in the sky of her brain. And still the pleasure continues as no one stops their teasing, biting, licking. It is his cry, as he comes deep into her throat, that brings a pause to the proceedings. His come first filling then sliding down her throat.

Scarlet slumps back against the wall. The soldier to her side pulls her close and holds her against his chest. Red lays her head on Scarlet's bare lap the musk of her pussy filling her tired senses.

The other two soldiers return to their bench. One lights both of their cigarettes from one match. The scene before him captivates him. He lights another match and bathes for those few seconds in their serenity.

Scarlet wakes, her legs folded under her, her head laying on her jacket folded to form the most comfortable pillow. She checks her watch. Its 7 a.m. They have gone. Every one of them. She thinks.

"Hello," no response, "Hello anyone there?" No response.

Her skirt has been laid over her waist and her blouse re-buttoned.

It all seems so un-real. Just maybe it was, but the taste in her mouth, the aches and bruises around her breasts and the beautiful throb in her pussy tells her otherwise.

She dresses then pushes the door open to be greeted by a young boy, handmade gun in his hand.

"Friend or foe," he shouts way too loudly with a mouth with its front teeth missing, a joy of life running through him.

Scarlet raises her hands in mock surrender.

"Friend, friend."

"Oh I'm sorry, love," the boy's mum comes from a nearby yard. "Terry leave the poor lady alone. Bad night last night eh, be bloody glad when this war is over."

The boy is ushered away as the woman doesn't even wait for her answer.

The area has been badly hit. Some houses, fortunately already abandoned, reduced to rubble heaps.

Slowly Scarlet regains her composure and follows, so far as she can, the route back to the main road to collect the bus home.

It is as she waits at the stop, her mind drifting to the events of the night before, that the military car pulls up before her.

The Red head steps out. It's her. Red.

"I've been asked to offer you a lift, ma'am."

The invitation is signed off with a clipped chassis, a sharp salute and then finally a soft slow wink. Red opens the door and Scarlet slides into the soft leather seats. They are there. All three of them. Seeing them properly, her violators for the first time.

"Good morning, madam, let us introduce ourselves...."

With that Red shuts the door behind Scarlet and with another adventure to be had, puts the car into first gear and pulls into the traffic.

The First Date

Like the demons that crawl from the dark corners of your bedroom when you cannot sleep, the anxiety now overwhelmed Scarlet as she sat alone in a secluded booth at the swanky Tamara's Bar, situated in the Grand Hotel.

She had been on an orthodox dating site for some weeks and had now tired of the rugby players who wanted to cosily watch DVD's after going to a game, the men who talked endlessly of their ex's and the ones who had miraculously appeared 10 years older and two stones heavier than their profile picture when they arrived for the first date.

It was Louisa who had mentioned the Spice Catcher website after one too many glasses of Pinot after work the Friday before last. Once home that night, and reinforced by the wine, she had kicked off her heels and taken advantage of the special offer to enrol for the first 48 hours for free.

Her eyes drawn to the huge array of faces, chests and cocks of those men seeking excitement with women. It had been 3 a.m. and a nearly empty second bottle, before she had closed the lid on the lap top and headed to bed in a deep but aroused sleep.

She had woken late with a start, the site having become a vague erotic blur that had clouded her sleep.

"Oh God no!"

She bravely chewed on toast that refused to be swallowed, as she remembered that she had indeed conceded at 2 a.m. to fill in and post her profile.

With more than a degree of hesitation she had logged on. The sense of mischief she had felt as she had uploaded the picture of her stockings and panties crumpled on her bedroom floor was now replaced with a sense of embarrassment – a warning to herself not to drink too much even if it was a Friday night.

To her surprise she had received 56 messages. By deleting those that only posted pictures of their erect body parts or those who had grunted like Neanderthal sperm donors she had quickly narrowed the possibles down to six. Of those her favourite had quickly become Ed.

She and Ed had now been mailing a full week and after much teasing and flirting they were finally due to meet.

Due to meet…He was already 15 minutes late when her phone had vibrated and his message had come through.

"Sorry, babe," it said, "just finished meeting couldn't text before. Hope you get this in time. Can you do Tuesday instead?"

Scarlet resisted the initial urge to tell him to fuck right off or even to ask whether his wife had refused to give him a pass – Scarlet had her suspicions. Instead she just downed the last of her wine and readied herself to leave.

It was then the barman appeared with the refill.

"Not for me thanks," she had said.

"It's not on the house, madam; it's a gift from someone I would suggest was an admirer."

"Who?" she enquired.

"They said not to say for now, Miss," he answered.

Scarlet felt the eyes of the bar boring into her like a potential murderer waiting to be unveiled by Poirot. She tried discretely scouring the room as she checked her make up in the compact but saw no obvious candidates.

She saw only one obvious solution, down another glass. Just as soon as her empty glass hit the table, a refilled one appeared.

"Madam."

"No thank you. Tell whoever bought it I am grateful but won't accept it unless they bring it in person."

"Funny they thought you'd say that, madam."

The barman left the glass. Ten, twenty, thirty seconds passed before Scarlet felt the shadow appear on her shoulder and the admirer finally sat opposite her.

This was certainly not what she had been expecting. She was perhaps 40, 10 years older than Scarlet. A classic redhead with pale freckled skin and piercing blue eyes. A slim figure with a firm but small natural chest.

"How much?" the redhead breathed.

"What?" The realisation that she had been mistaken for a hooker both bewildered and shocked Scarlet.

"For the night?"

"I think there's been…"

"I pay extra for tricks but not coyness sweetness – how much?"

Scarlet's head started to buzz like a wasp in a fog flying around her skull. She had been on a high at the thought of Ed, then a low thinking of that disappointment but now here was this beautiful redhead thinking she was a call girl. She had its true a vague thought that one day in the right circumstances she might try a girl but shit, this wasn't for real.

"Okay let's play this a different way honey. Show me what I'm buying. £10 for each of the first three buttons then £30 for each of the next three."

Maybe it was the wine. The wine that had started to fuzz her fears and caution and now made her toes and pussy tingle. Maybe those grapes had frazzled her enough to play just a little but even Scarlet hadn't expected to hear the next words escape her mouth.

"Show me the money."

The woman reached in her trouser pocket and pulled a pile of notes. She counted three £10 notes into one pile and nine £10 notes into a second.

"Well?" redhead breathed again.

The first three buttons were easy money but the next three would leave her bare to the woman in front of her. She took another gulp of the wine and let it run through her. She breathed deep. Did she really want this?

Scarlet felt her breasts fill and her nipples harden as she slowly reached down and let the fourth, fifth then sixth button release itself from its anchor.

"Show me."

"I can't not here."

"I said show me," The woman's eyes smouldered and her breathing deepened.

Scarlet checked her angles from 90 degrees forward. She was confident no one could see. Slowly she peeled her blouse back till the full swell of her breasts and hardened pink nipples were in full view.

"Delicious," growled redhead, "stay just like that," she laid out a further £50 on the table.

"Ready?"

"Ready for?" Scarlet said sounding considerably braver than she felt.

Red reached slowly across the small table that separated them, her eyes locking with Scarlet's. Scarlet felt herself powerless to resist the soft sweet breath as Red first teased then fed her lips as they softly engaged. A soft fingertip massaging the top of Scarlet's nipple. Scarlet breathed hard as Red disengaged, almost disappointed she had not been offered more.

"Disappointed?" Red guessed. "Good now I know you want me. £500 for the night. You coming?"

"Yes," the words leapt from Scarlet's mouth.

"You can close two buttons. I pick the first and sixth."

Scarlet knew as she rose that anyone who looked side on would see virtually her full bosom and hardened nipples. Even the otherwise discrete barman who they passed on the way out smiled and wished them a fun evening.

The journey to the lift was surreal. The journey in the lift from the first to the 10th floor more so as Red slipped Scarlet's skirt up over her hips to her waist and stroked the gentle area between her arse cheeks, as the young Italian couple looked on.

The pace of their march to Red's room was relentless slowing only as she pushed Scarlet hard against the outside of her bedroom door and raped her mouth with her tongue as she searched deep inside her pockets for the key.

"The money," Scarlet had blurted shortly before Red closed the door and faced her.

Red scowled leaving Scarlet to believe a punishment was to come before the notes were placed on the table.

"Ready now?" Red sarcastically growled.

The buttons of Scarlet's blouse flew like shrapnel across the room as it was ripped from her. Her thighs nearly burned as her skirt only partially undone was pulled down her thighs and she was pushed firmly on her back onto the huge bed.

The gentle tongue that teased Scarlet through the silk of her crotch sent shivers to every G spot. She tried to resist, tried to detach but the soft wet mouth seduced her, first through the material then bare as the panties followed her skirt.

The mouth like a wall of wet warmth folding itself around her clit. The sharp snaky tongue slowly breaking through her guarding, reddened lips before flicking soft long circles around her clit.

The throbbing grew slowly, grew heavier. Scarlet's mind wondered to far distant and forbidden pockets of ill-gotten desire. Still the tongue worked. A woman's tongue softer more caressing than a man's, with its slow soft massaging strokes.

Scarlet's orgasm took her by surprise, as she shuddered and released her juices deep into the woman's waiting mouth.

As Scarlet gathered her breath, as the heat flowed through her, she sensed Red undressing. Just as her breathing returned to normal she is offered a petite breast with a long hard almost red nipple, fed to her like a child. Her mouth opening and suckling hard in response to the groan above her. Her tummy now straddled by Red's bare thighs. Feeling her wet pussy staining Scarlet's bare vulnerable midriff, the pussy rolling itself along her tummy as her mouth feeds on Red's breasts. The thighs now rubbing across Scarlet's breasts as slowly Red's pussy hovers within a tongue reach of Scarlet. Her first taste of a woman.

Like a child prompted to taste food for the first time Scarlet's tongue is hesitant, maybe overly gentle but the hesitancy excites Red who controls the pressure by lowering herself or heightening herself on Scarlet's tongue. The feeling is delicious. The realisation that Red's pleasure is now in her control empowers Scarlet.

She feels Red's thighs shake, her breath quicken, and her clit harden. She climaxes deep and hard clamping her thighs tightly around Scarlet's head.

For the first time a pause, a truce.

Scarlet surprises herself by making the next move. A gentle kiss, soft at first then harder until Red's mouth opens deeply to receive her searching tongue. Red readily concedes and presses herself forward as Scarlet's tongue searches out her hardened nipples and bare exposed neck and shoulders. Then her tummy and again her pussy lips, dressed in her flame red shaped pussy hair.

Her thighs spread wide and the searching gentle tongue feeds first on the love juice leaking deeply from Red then on the silky smooth clit that renders Red to a helpless sexual puppet.

Red's cry rings loud around the room and they hold each other tight as the climax shudders, jerks then trembles to a gentle close.

Their eyes slowly focus on each other and they kiss softly, gently, before Red whispers almost without thinking "one more treat."

Scarlet lays back her tired vision lazily regarding the light fitting above her before she feels the nudge at her mouth of Red's cock, the strap on one now fixed to her waist.

"Suck me, wet me?" she almost pleads.

Scarlet takes it deep like a cock until satisfied by some invisible test, Red pulls it from her and gentle nudges it against Scarlet's pussy.

It enters virtually without resistance. Harder than a man. The thrusts are strong and deep, inch by inch filling Scarlet. Soon each thrust fills her, crashing hard into her g spot, harder, faster, harder, faster.

Scarlet hears her cry echo across the room and scream back at her as her orgasm is released to the world.

She can barely rest before Red forces the cock into her mouth and Scarlet cleans her of her own juices.

They sleep in an exhausted embrace, tired fingers stroking the other, soft kisses dressing their shoulders, soft bites of the others midriff.

The alarm scares Scarlet into the real world. Its 5 a.m. and Red already showered and dressed leans above her.

"Sorry, baby, I have to go. The rooms paid for sleep tight."

"But..."

"You'll see me again don't worry."

"But I don't even know your name."

"It's Edwina – my friends call me Ed, babe."
With that Ed winks, smiles and leaves.

Gravy

He used to love her. He couldn't sleep for thinking of her. He couldn't breathe for thinking of her. Resorting even to following her home from a night out with her girlfriends to see if there was someone else, so fearsome had he been of losing her.

But now 10 years later they barely connected. Oh she still kissed his cheek when he came home from work and asked dutifully how his day had been as she laid the table around him. Yes, she still bought out his favourite roast dinner for his Friday night treat but he knew he had reaped what he had sown.

Years of trying to make her his had left him with somebody he simply didn't want.

Now more handsome than pretty, and maybe a stone heavier than when they had met he regarded her now as he did his vinyl record collection. He couldn't bear to part with it but had no interest in playing it.

With a brief smile between them he puts another morsel of his delicious roast beef in his mouth and lets it melt slowly.

He thinks briefly of Alice, the young secretary who had recently joined his vast insurance company, and looks forward to the start of Gardeners' World.

She looks at him and see's everything that makes the anger rise within her. The way he chews his beef, his patronising smile, the way that he thinks of the young girls in his office. She thinks back to when she had been so pretty that she could have had any boy she wanted. When he used to follow her home. Check her mobile phone. Check her address book. Smothered her of her friends until they abandoned her.

She chews her beef quietly and slowly. Her small mouth closes around the soft meat. And she smiles. The thought of her mouth closed around soft meat makes her smile because that's not how it was just two hours ago.

When she had been with him, her young lover. The one she had seen for two years now. The one who still kisses her like it was their first kiss. The one who she fears will rip the buttons from her blouse in his desire to see her breasts. The one who licks her pussy like a programmed vibrator such that she comes deep on his beautiful young face. Comes so deeply that her juices coat him like a thin, sexual varnish.

Then he had forced her mouth around his young hard cock, sliding her throat along its full length. Making her suck him harder and harder before he had pushed her onto her all fours and thrust himself deep inside her.

Then he had fucked her hard. Hard and fast. She had breathed deep and moaned so loudly as he had twitched, jerked and called her name out loud as he buried his come deep, deep inside her.

And so she now sits opposite him, her husband, at the dining room table. Him – with his barely concealed venom. Her with her lover's come leaking deep in her knickers.

And she smiles enigmatically but inside she laughs, laughs so loud.

"Gravy, dear?" She asks.

The Black Death

We were the Black Death. A ship decommissioned from her Navy by the Queen of England so that we could with others, haunt and torment the French and Spanish.

So successful had we been in plundering his trading ships that Louis the fearsome King of Spain, had sent a small fleet of six galleons to rid the seas of us once and for all.

For weeks we had managed to avoid direct contact with them, and had continued to plunder the smaller ships of their stocks of tobacco, wine and treasure.

But now their net was closing around us. We had spotted the first of them to our right as the sun rose at first light. Then the second to our left. Soon we were in the centre of their web. There was no chance of outrunning them, these were the best and fastest ships the Spanish had. There was no chance of out fighting them, each of their ships had three times more armour than us. There was no chance of surrender, we would all be hung from the highest mast.

I am Captain Black. My first mate is Scarlet Kiss, the dutiful niece of the King of France when I captured her, but now with her depraved ways and fearlessness in the face of battle, she has long since been disowned by him and is now as wanted as me and the rest of my crew. She is also now my wife. But as we sit sharpening our swords and cleaning our pistols it looks like our adventure is set for an explosive but fatal climax.

The plan seemed impossible and without the little bottle of magic we had been given by the Queen of Persia, it would have been. I take no credit for it. It was Smythe the young daughter of the head of supplies who suggested it. If the Queen of Persia was true to her word, the magic potion would allow the entire crew to morph into the ship giving the impression to all who came across her that she was entirely deserted.

The Queen of Persia's word was good and within the hour the good ship, the Black Death, was deserted. Its floorboard creaking, its sails billowing in the wind.

I watched as they approached. I sat on the highest sail. To the Spanish I was but a black crow, the single inhabitant of the ship. Excited Spanish accents soon filled the air. With the little Spanish language I had picked up on my travels, I hear their calls to blast our ship to matchwood. To rid the seas of the Black Death once and for all. But they do not.

It is Scarlet who has morphed into the figurehead at the front of the ship that has drawn their attention. That has saved us all.

A soft melancholic mermaid song drifts from her filling the sailor's ears.

So beautiful is the figurehead that the Admiral of the fleet himself feels bound to come see. Heading the party that boards our ship he walks on the planks that surround the figurehead to face Scarlet. His lust for her is overwhelming.

I caw into the air and hop onto the bow of the ship behind him so like him, I am looking at Scarlet.

He strokes her breasts and tummy before sliding his fingers between her legs, resting softly on her hood.

And therein lies the one failing of the magic potion. Whilst to the outside world she is a beautiful wooden carving, Scarlet can feel every touch as if it was her own bare flesh.

The Admiral's hands are soft and skilful. He delights in his new wooden toy, so life like is it.

Even her hood seems to open under his fingers. The volume of her mermaid song increasing with her arousal.

The song drives his passion like a voice from the God's validating his violation of the figurehead.

He looks deep into Scarlet's eyes and kisses her soft mouth. So sure is he that her tongue searches out his, he kisses her deeper.

I look on at this violation of my wife. Knowing she can feel every touch of his fingers. The saliva on his tongue. The surge of violence that rages through me is tempered by a perverse pleasure. One I cannot easily explain.

The Captains of the surrounding ships fear for his sanity, as the man who leads them continues his foreplay with the wooden beauty.

But within her trapped form, Scarlet is gasping. His long manicured fingers delve through the hood and slowly and softly massage her clit. He is pressed so hard against her that Scarlet can feel his long hard cock burning into her flat tummy.

The song becomes louder seducing the ears of all who hear it. So seducing the crews that no one notices the mist that starts to surround each Galleon at sea level.

The Admiral's mouth now sucks at Scarlet's neck, ears and shoulders. Biting and sucking on the wooden skin convinced in himself that he feels it give under his weight.

Then his mouth folding around her long hard aching brown wooden nipples. The nipples he swears harden yet further in his mouth.

I watch intently. I cannot risk Scarlet's life or that of my crew by returning to my human state and wreaking death on this man but that anger is in part aimed at me. For the pleasure I enjoy. Knowing she is with this stranger. Trapped and enclosed, powerless to resist him. Her debauched mind and body giving in slowly as I knew it would to this physical pleasure.

Many of the Captains and crew turn from him in their shame as he loosens his breaches and strokes his glistening helmet against her slit. The slit that needs no lubrication from the pre come that flows from him, soaking with her love juice, as it already is.

The helmet pressed hard against her until it slides past her resistance. The cock so thick that it stretches her tiny cunt.

Inside Scarlet groans and begs him to fuck her hard. Her cunt filled like never before. But to them, the mermaid song just sounds louder and more beautiful. So beautiful the clouds gather and swirl in circles above their heads.

The Admirals hips start to roll and buck. He can feel her muscles grip and spasm around his shaft.

The Captains and crews watch on, sensibilities fudged as their leader pounds his cock into the wooden figurehead.

My head is hurting. Seeing how his huge cock has stretched my tiny wife. Knowing how she is surrendering to him. Even I do not want to see this stop, though I cannot reason why.

The Admiral is sure he sees just a flicker in her eyes, hears a small pant escape her lips. Driving his effort, his hands grip Scarlet's breasts as tightly as he can. The grip helping him to drive even more of his thick cock inside her.

Scarlet fears she will lose consciousness. Her breasts ache, a deep hurtful throb. Never before has her cunt been so stretched that she fears she may tear.

Her song now fully bewitching the crews of the surrounding ships. The shame they initially felt of his violation of this figurehead turning to jealousy. Jealousy that it is him not them fucking her. A feeling that arouses me even more. Wondering in my head how it would feel for them to queue and take her one by one.

Their Captains now wary of the changing mood. The hint of mutiny and rebellion.

But the Admiral does not notice. He is so enraptured that he just pumps his cock into her, faster and harder.

Scarlet comes deep on his shaft flooding him with her come. He feels it too.

"She is coming," he yells across the sea. My stomach rolls as a wave of nausea rolls through me.

And he in turn erupts inside of her. Jets of his hot come first filling her then spurting from her as he continues to thrust.

The orgasm rushes through her body, teasing her pleasure receptors, making her tingle and burn like tiny electric shocks.

It is only he who sees her head slump slightly as Scarlet tries to gulp in air in her restricted shell.

He leans into her ear. "Thank you," he whispers.

The sight is though quite beautiful. I know Scarlet well enough to know that she is aching with pleasure. Desperate for more. Battered but never broken.

A cloak is thrown around the Admiral's shoulders. He is led to the rowing boat which will take him to his cabin where he will drink freely on brandy and dream of the figurehead.

The Captains of the other ships see the mutiny in the mood of their crews. They order extra rum rations to ease the tension and mood. It works as before long their stories turn from the events of the day to ones of whores and orgies and plunder and pillage.

We wait and listen. So much does Scarlet desire to slide her fingers over her come coated clit or plunge her fingers into her come filled hole.

But she doesn't.

None of my crew move or turn back into our human form. I monitor the Spanish flying briefly from ship to ship. Just watching.

We wait till darkness falls and the only sound louder than the snoring of the crew lying unconscious on the decks is the sound of an empty rum bottle sliding from one side of the deck to the other in time with the tide.

She smiles and I smile as once again we become Scarlet and Black, the best Pirates who sail the sea.

With our crew now armed, we board the Admiral's ship as the other five are sunk by cannon fire before their crew have time to come to their senses.

It is strange that amongst the chaos, the Admiral seems pleased to see us.

He looks into Scarlet's eyes and touches her lips with his soft fingers. He smiles a reassuring and collusional smile as he sees the wet patch of his come still soaking into Scarlet's breaches.

"Thank you," is again all he says as I slip the noose around his slender neck.

The Wife's Revenge?

You know him so well, those tell-tale signs.

The new pay as you go phone you found in his suit. The way he shuts down the page on his computer as you approach. The odd night out with the friends from work he has never mentioned before.

You would love to say it's the last straw, but the straw broke the camel's back long ago. It is time for him to walk, but not before you have had your revenge.

It's not so hard to find the sex site he is on. Sitting him with his laptop and his back to the mirror in the lounge was easy enough. You fill in your profile and add a picture of your stockinged legs. You will be Scarlet.

Now the search. Males within 5 miles. Too many options, although you deliberate a little too long looking at the cock pictures. Okay 2 miles and 5 years either way of his age. Bingo! You quickly check his profile. Same height, town, age, cock size, band, etc. It's a match.

You check his special interests. He seeks sex outdoors with strangers. Interesting!

The plan starts to evolve. It is all so easy. The way of introduction is to send a wink. You send one, then a second. He bites. His first message.

"Hi what are you looking for?

"How novel," You reply – "I want someone to make love to my mind before they make love to my body. Outdoors preferred. No pre meetings. Just get it on."

His next message genuinely surprises you. It is vivid, exciting and frankly Goddam horny. Well I never you smile to yourself. The flirtation continues for a week or so. He asks for your e-mail address. You refuse to provide it. He asks for a phone number. Once you have bought your own pay as you go phone you give the number to him. His is the only one on it!

Finally you feel ready. You wait till he is online then go upstairs to your own laptop and mail him on the site.

"I am so horny. I want to be fucked now" you message.

"Tell me you are serious" he responds.

"I don't joke when I'm this horny – are you free?" you tempt.

"Can be where and when?" he almost too eagerly responds.

"Nine o'clock the secluded lay-by off Smith's Lane – do you know it?"

Of course you know he knows it.

"Cool," he says. "I will flash my headlights so you know it's me."

At 8.30 he tells you he is going out for a beer. You smell the fresh breath where he has just cleaned his teeth. You tell him to have fun. Now just catching him there would be fun but you want to push this revenge to the limit. To the stage where he thinks he can have you.

Having already showered, you quickly mount the stairs and put on your best bra and knickers and a see through wrap over dress you have bought some weeks before. You tuck your hair into the short black bob wig you purchased for an upcoming fancy dress party then head off.

You drive to the lay-by. It is turning from dusk to dark. The nerves start to kick in. You chew mint gum to keep your breath fresh and wipe your sweating hands on the small towel you keep as a precaution by the dashboard. You check as cars go by to see what they might be able to see of the lay-by.

The flashing headlights from the front take you by surprise.

"Shit he's here early," you exclaim loudly but to yourself.

You flash back. The text message arrives.

"Evening, Scarlet. I wasn't sure you would come."

"I told you I was horny" you reply.

Whilst the message is confident the fingers that type it tremble slightly. The next message.

"Get out of the car I want to see you," he says.

You wonder at what point he will realise it is you. What will he notice first – a mole, a freckle? You check the wig then put on the non-prescription glasses you purchased that day and finish the look with a slick of red lipstick. You exit the car and slowly tread so that you stand with your back to the bonnet. The scene reminiscent of the prisoner exchanges in gangster or old cold war movies where the headlights of the car blinds the eyes of the other. The next message. You check your phone.

"Open the dress and lay back on the bonnet."

In a funny way this suits you. He will have to be right by you before he looks into your eyes. What you had not banked on, though, is the thrill. The sexual tension has been building in every muscle. Almost fuelled by vengeance you are starting to feel aroused, wet and distinctly in a mood to be fucked senseless. If only this was for real. You hear a car door open and close, then his footsteps. Closer and closer. A hand touches your bare leg. The hand is cool compared to the warmth of the engine on your back. It glides almost tenderly along your calves, then inner thigh, then lightly over the silk knickers covering your pussy. The touch so light like when you first met. He slides your knickers over your hips down your legs and over the ankles. You still can't see him but then neither can he see your face. You feel his lips slowly making their way along your thighs.

A small cog in the nagging section of your brain tells you something is wrong. There is something wrong, but you don't know what it is. Oh God there is a watch on his arm. HE doesn't have a watch!

"Scarlet, you are beautiful."

The voice is not his. You have it wrong. This really is a stranger.

The moment hangs in the air like cigarette smoke on a frosty day. The second before you act seems like an hour. Even then the dominant instruction in your brain to immediately seek the safety of the car comes out as little more than a whimper as he gently kisses the soft skin of your guarding lips. And again. And again. It is such an intimate moment with a complete stranger. One more intimate than you have had with HIM for what seems forever. He stops and stands before you.

"Are you okay, Scarlet?" he says with a gentle voice. "You seem unsure."

This is your moment. He is giving you the opportunity to walk away now. He doesn't know your real name or where you live. You can just put this behind you.

But there is something about the moment. The chance to have this surreal anonymous erotic experience. You are just so, so horny now.

His eyes blue and twinkling show a genuine concern.

"I'm fine," you hear the alien occupying your body say.

He leans to you and kisses the corner of each side of your lips then your nose then tugs tenderly at your bottom lip with his teeth. His tongue now gently probing inside. Your tongue is now also occupied by the alien and it starts to dance with his. Harder and harder. You feel the air running out and pull away to catch your breath.

"Phew," he says smiling.

You smile back. His teeth and lips work their way from the silky soft skin behind your ear along your neck to your chest. Unclipping your bra his mouth works over the mound of your breast then takes in your nipple. His teeth gripping its shaft, the tip of his tongue teasing the tip. You can feel it growing stiffer and stiffer. Then his tongue working along your tummy till it rests at the tip of your pussy lips.

"I…" you try to say as a final protest but your thoughts are lost as his fingers gently part your hood and his tongue touches your bare exposed hard clit. His expert tongue first flicks and then massages you. You can feel the heat spreading across your pussy and picture the view he has of your now swollen, very red pussy. His tongue delves to the sweet musky nectar now freely flowing from you and takes his coated tongue along the silky precious skin between your entrance and clit then to your clit itself.

"Oh fuck yes," you moan.

You can hear your words rising into the air, then the long moan which follows straight after as the intense heat rushes through you. The deep almost painful waves follow, drowning the intense throbbing in your clit. He doesn't stop but carries on although more slowly and gently now. The orgasm still washing through you for what seems minutes. Finally it subsides. Your thighs tremble and your limp back slumps against the bonnet. He again kisses your hood gently then works his way along to your body till his tongue and yours dance a rampant tango in your mouth.

You both start as a car pulls alongside. You feel a deep weight hit your tummy fearing a plain clothes police patrol but then you recognise the car. It's HIS. The window rolls down. He has the internal light on and has a female passenger by his side.

"What a fantastic show," he says. "I hope you don't mind but we saw the lights flashing and pulled in."

A second or so passes before you realise he has no idea who you are. After all the years you have been together, he does not know your body your legs, your face behind the glasses, anything.

"Do you mind if we watch?" You have made me really horny," he carries on."

"No, mate," says your lover carefully covering your breasts to protect your modesty "I don't think so."

You rise to his ear. "Let him," you whisper. "Let's put on a show."

You slide from the bonnet onto your haunches and take out your lover's already stiff cock. The taste of his pre come drifts into your taste buds. He lets you take control and your tongue massages the filament under his knob before gradually your tight mouth takes in more and more of his shaft. Alternating between teeth and lips your mouth works faster and faster. Your hand massages and then more tightly grips his balls. You can feel them tightening. But this is not how you will allow him to come. Oh no, by a twist of fate the final act of revenge is close. You turn, slide your front over the bonnet and offer your lover your abused wet entrance.

"Fuck me hard and rough," you say.

You look across at him. His passenger is wanking him hard. Oh the irony of him getting off on his little wife from home being fucked in front of his own eyes by a total stranger. Your lover is now deep inside you. He is holding your hips and is fucking you like the piston on a steam engine.

"Fuck me fuck me," You moan.

HE does not even recognise your voice as his pleasure now takes him over, his orgasm betrayed by his rolling eyes. Your Lover moans. His pelvic bone helping to bring you to your second orgasm as it slaps against your clit. The fatal twitch and jerk and you can feel the hot come flood your cavern. A stranger's hot come deep inside you. Your Lover pulls you to him and you kiss again. This time as consummation of the pleasure you have shared. By the time you part and have regained your breath, HE and the car have left.

Your senses are in overdrive as you make your way to your front door. A sense of hedonistic wild abandon floods through your brain whilst a gentle throbbing still teases your pussy. The last of the strangers come seeping into the gusset of your knickers.

HE is not home. You look at yourself in the hall mirror and smile. As a souvenir of HIS night you leave your wig, glasses and come soaked knickers on his laptop.

You are nearly asleep when you hear his key open the front door and he none too quietly tip toes to his laptop in the lounge. A smile spreads across your lips as you hear his words.

"What the fuck..."

The Auction

"I will post a picture of you on a sex site. You may wear an opera mask or some such to conceal your identity if you choose but otherwise your outfit will consist of elbow length gloves, small black thong, heels and bondage tape covering your breasts. You will be put up for sale. The bid will last for 24 hours. The highest bid gets you providing it reaches £5,000. If that figure is not reached you have no obligation to go. If it is they have you for 5 hours – no more. I will set out the terms upon which they can use you."

Scarlet's fling with Matt had hit many highs in the three months they had been together but this was a considerable leap from their other cautionary adventures.

True, Scarlet had in hindsight perhaps foolishly asked what it was that she could do for Matt's birthday that none of the other girls in his life had ever done, but the visual image she had conjured of her jumping scantily clad from a birthday cake was clearly not imaginative enough for Matt.

Scarlet was not a swinger, well not yet at least. However, with each small step she had taken with Matt she found herself much more in tune with her inner pervert. From those early days of watching porn with Matt, to their first public sex and then the first film they had made together, she had found an as yet un-satiated desire to be used, pleasured abused and satisfied. Each experience being a small step on a path to the complete hedonistic experience.

But this…

"You are kidding right, Matt?" she had text.

"Err no – you asked me what I wanted for my birthday," he had replied.

"But you do know for that sort of money the winner is going to want to have sex with me right?" she thought stating the obvious might bring Matt to his senses.

"I bloody hope so, I don't want to watch you doing his ironing."

"So you want me to have sex with a stranger whilst you watch?"

"Yep that's just about it, beautiful – the best present I could wish for."

"Yeah good luck with that, fuck wit," she had texted.

Neither had texted the other in the succeeding 24 hours.

The cooling off period affected them both in quite different ways. Whereas Matt had let sink in the reality of watching Scarlet be used and fucked by another man, Scarlet had so warmed to the idea that she had already masturbated herself to a state of virtual exhaustion.

"I'm so sorry, love. I was being an idiot. Please forget I ever suggested it," Matt had finally texted.

"I'll do it," was Scarlet's response.

"You'll what?"

"I'll do it, if that's what you want, seeing me fucked by a stranger, then that is what you will get."

"But I'm not sure that's what I do want now..."

As each sat on their own chairs in their own homes with their phones in their hands, their swaying emotions clashed hard with their sexual desires.

Message after message exchanged, Scarlet knew how Matt felt. As much as his driven lust longed to see her used by a stranger, she recognised his fear that their relationship might be changed forever. The dream of your girlfriend as a whore, fucked by another man, might be very different to actually being with one. Scarlet herself could feel the same nauseating stab of the dagger as she wondered how she might feel if it was he who was to play.

The texts had turned to a late and long phone call. A call that had become lubricated with wine, and their shared views of how horny it would be if Scarlet went through with it. They had each masturbated to climax and agreed in an excited orgasm it should go ahead – besides who would bid £5,000.

The photos they posted showed Scarlet as Matt saw her. Her stunning blue eyes pierced the slits of the opera mask like lasers, her soft perfectly formed lips, dressed in red and pouting like a soft breath.

Having each read the message several times Matt dinked the post key and their message appeared on line.

The site enabled them to monitor how many people were viewing the message. The number soon rose from tens to hundreds.

The inevitable time waster messages followed. Requests for sight of Scarlet fully bare before a member would decide to bid being the most common.

A few admonitions too from those more kind hearted members being concerned that Scarlet was being sold against her will. But as the hours wore on and the number of watching members stood firm, the bids slowly started to roll in.

Matt had cleverly set up a graph chart with a column set up for each bidder with each square measuring bids in units of £100.

By the seventh hour they retired to bed with the figure at £2,500. After a fitful sleep and three cups of coffee it had reached £4,250.

It had to be said that by the 22nd hour Scarlet was only remotely attracted to one of the bidders – the other two appearing to be that type of self-made man with money, no real friends and a dominant mother. Her heart sank further when after 23 hours and fifty minutes her preferred choice dropped from the race leaving only the other two.

But then a new bid. The bidder without photos or profile named only as the Gentleman's Club of St Augustin. A chill kangarooed the length of her spine like a nervous learner driver as Scarlet repeated their name out loud.

"Fuck me," whispered Matt, as the sum of £7,500 flicked into the graph.

A message popped into the inbox.

"We make this offer on the strict basis that what is said in the bidding prospectus is true – you assure us it is?" – Christopher of the Gentleman's Club.

Nervously Scarlet and Matt re-read their message.

"An auction. My beautiful girlfriend as pictured new to these pleasures and games but keen to learn and please. The best offer received in 24 hours providing it exceeds £5,000 will win her for up to five hours. This game is for our joint pleasure so I will watch. No timewasters please. No further photos will be provided. Payment required in cleared funds before play commences."

"I assure you it is," Matt replies.

"We hold you to that, Christopher."

As they reach the 24th hour the bid from the Gentleman's Club is the narrow but clear winner.

Scarlet takes a long gulp from her wine glass and goes to sit on the edge of her bed whilst Matt mails Christopher to confirm payment terms.

His initial comment that it's all probably a spoof brings a sheepish look to his face as his online Bank statement confirms receipt of the payment within 20 minutes.

Scarlett is told that the Gentleman's Club will make final arrangements through Matt. He is sworn to secrecy and refuses to budge or concede to every form of provocation, lure or pout Scarlet can throw at him.

She is told only three things:

The meeting will take place this coming Saturday when a car will collect her at 7 p.m. and drive her to her destination. Matt will text her at 7.15 p.m. with a safe word she has agreed with him to confirm it is safe and he is in place.

She needs to be showered but not perfumed.

She can wear whatever she wants – she will be dressed when she arrives.

The week passes without further contact and the day of the meeting finally arrives. They both realise an unspoken tension lies deep between them no matter how much they both try to act as normally as possible. A slight tetchiness, each catching the other watching them in silent thought, the sentences that are started but not finished.

By six Matt has showered and dressed.

"Are you sure, love?" he says one last time. "It's not too late, it never is."

"I want to, darling," Scarlet comforts as she kisses his cheek. "It's just a game, just fun. Promise me you will enjoy watching and keep me safe."

"The safe word is 'birthday'. Text me at any time and its cancelled okay? Shout it at any time and it's finished."

"Then I'll say it now, darling, happy birthday."

They kiss softly then Matt leaves.

The house seems so empty in that last hour. Scarlet showers and slowly applies her make-up electing for a look that mirrors the picture that Matt posted on the site. She dresses in her favourite mid-thigh black cocktail dress, simple black bra and knickers and black heels. Then she sits and sits and waits and waits. Only ever but a moment from texting the word 'birthday', to Matt.

Her nerve nearly cracks but as she reaches for the phone there is a small but distinctive knock at the door.

"Evening, madam, my name is Tinto, I am your driver for the evening."

Scarlet draws a breath. The driver smells of old money, of respectful servitude.

"Are you okay?" he asks reassuringly, seeing her nervous features.

"Yes of course," she lies.

By the time her senses can readjust Scarlet is in the car, humming smoothly towards its secret destination.

Scarlet tries to follow the route being taken by Tinto but the car is soon travelling through dark unfamiliar country roads and her mind instead wanders to the evening ahead. Ahead to the mysterious Christopher and his Gentleman's Club.

Her trance is broken by Matt's text.

"All fine here. Remember the safe word is birthday – enjoy. Matt X."

She cannot know the mixed emotions Matt has experienced in sending that text. Even now as his cock hardens at the thought of Scarlet being used by another, the feelings of pending jealousy rage through him. The almost despair within him of seeing her face in ecstasy at the hands of this stranger. Yet the lust will win out. He knows that now. He holds his breath awaiting Scarlet's response.

"I will. Hope you do, too. On my way S x."

Scarlet is nervous but not for the same reasons as Matt. He has given her license to play. There is no guilt, no jealousy. No her nervousness comes from that anticipation that can only come from a sexual meeting with a complete stranger. Paid sex. She will tonight be a stranger's paid whore.

The thought which should rankle her feminist sensitivities instead sends a deep tingle through her already damp pussy.

The car slows as Tinto steers the car onto a long gravel path. The silhouette of a large 1920s style house looms in Scarlet's eye line. Dimly lit. Imposing.

"This is mad," Scarlet tells herself. "Absolutely fucking barking."

She is glad of the cool autumn air as Tinto opens her door. He escorts her through the dimly lit garden area leading to what seems to be a tradesman's entrance. The irony is not lost on Scarlet. A small tap on the doorknocker, feet shuffling, then the door opens.

"Evening, madam, please follow me," says the waiting figure. Scarlet feels no desire for small talk and simply follows the man through a small maze of wood panelled corridors, dressed with portraits of long forgotten military types before he stops outside a door.

"The Master asks that you change in here. When you are ready please leave through the other door where the members will greet you."

Members, Members. The emphasis on the plural rings around Scarlet's head as she closes the door to the changing room behind her. Whilst she of course knew this was a Club the thought had simply not occurred to her that there would be more than one participant.

How many were there? Would they be watching like a theatre? Her brain raced as she slowly stepped from her dress, bra and panties.

The outfit she is required to wear seems to her to be entirely unsexy. A black sheer blouse, barely long enough to cover her bottom and simple sheer black tights with a heavy black gusset. She slips on her black heels and after a deep breath leaves through the other door.

The room is so dark that even after 30 seconds her eyes can still make out no discernible shapes.

"I am glad you could join us, Scarlet. I wasn't entirely sure you would. Please turn around briefly for me then we can start."

The voice has that tone of authority. That tone where a request seems like a command that cannot be refused. As Scarlet turns 180 degrees, she hears a door open behind her and others enter the room. The sound of expectant bodies settling into leather armchairs. How many? Five maybe six?

"You may turn around now, Scarlet, so we may all see you properly."

A dim light falls upon her from the ceiling illuminating her to the members. A chorus of muttered approvals. The smell of cologne now reaches her nose. Of the members she can see little. The dim light enables her to see that they are seated in a semi-circle. A match is struck, then another, briefly lighting up a face as a cigar is lit. The smoke curls into the air.

"You know the safe word Scarlet. Use it if you must."

There is the brief ring of a butler bell and a figure enters from the changing room. A woman. A beautiful woman. Older maybe 40. Her eyes lock on Scarlet's but there is no smile, no acknowledgement.

With a flick of her wrist the woman opens a flick knife, the blade glinting in the light. The point of the blade is pressed into Scarlet's tummy, blade up. Slowly, oh so slowly, the woman slices through the thread holding each button, then steers the blouse from Scarlet's shoulders to the floor. Her pert breasts now on full view, her small pink nipples harden under the appreciative gazes. Her breasts like her pussy now aching with a need to be used.

The woman circles Scarlet and kneeling from behind cuts a small hole in the gusset of the tights then using her hands rips the rear of the gusset to shreds. She crawls slowly to front Scarlet. Scarlet feels the blunt side of the blade nestled between her sex lips through the material, she cannot help but murmur her pleasure.

The blade cuts through the gusset and the woman frenziedly tears at the material jerking Scarlet like a rag doll in the process. The woman rises to her feet to admire her handy work. Scarlet can feel her bare shaved pussy now entirely exposed and on view.

With her eyes locked with Scarlet's the woman lets the blade of the knife trace its way across Scarlet's tensed tummy, then the mounds of her breasts coming to rest against the stalk of her right nipple.

The frission of fear, that she may be cut, makes Scarlet groan with lust. The sharp pain. The small cut is made an inch to the right of the nipple and brings tiny speckles of blood to the surface. The woman leans down and lets her tongue trace across Scarlet's nipple then folds her mouth around the wound sucking and licking it clean.

Scarlet feels her juices leaking freely onto her upper thighs, the sweet musk filling the air.

The woman rises and smiles for the first time.

"Come with me," she says.

A low diffused light falls onto an altar just a few feet behind them. Scarlet is guided up two short steps until she is positioned on its stage on her knees but torso erect.

Her arms are raised above her head and her wrists cuffed from chains hanging from the ceiling. The chains are pulled tighter so her body is now held taut.

She hears movement beneath her like a door sliding but cannot look down to see. More matches are struck, faces briefly seen, and more perfumed smoke fills the room.

She can feel the heavy presence of the woman behind her, then hears a flurry of swishes. The heat sears across her back as in a swirl of her wrists the woman lets loose with her two mini floggers.

Beyond play spanking with Matt, Scarlet had never been subjected to pain for pleasure but here, now, fully bared for her audience, all modesty and nerves abandoned, she lets her mind slowly absorb the image of herself in the members' eyes.

With each small blow the pain gradually morphs into a deep satisfying heat. The floggers now on her front, initially randomly, but gradually weaving into a focussed assault on her breasts and pussy.

The almost unbearable pain wielding to heat then replaced in turn by an ache, a deeply sensual sexual ache linking her inflamed sensitive nipples to her wet throbbing pussy.

She feels more signs of the growing orgasm building within her. The blows no longer identifiable individually but now one single assault on her sex. The waves stronger deeper than she could ever remember – craving release. And then that moment, that blow against her hood that drives her over the edge. Her grunt of release fills the room as her juices smear the mirrored surface beneath her – the heat surging through her loins and thighs.

Now whimpering her wrists are released and she sinks onto all fours, still twitching as the aftershocks take control of her body.

"Quite beautiful, Scarlet, mesmerising," the commanding voice praises "Now please stay just like that whilst we join you."

Still catching her breath Scarlet raises her head to see the five figures approaching her. She feels her bottom cheeks parted and a tongue, the woman's, gently start to flick and tease her anus.

The thousands of nerve endings there send electrolytes of pleasure around Scarlet's body. She sees the men reaching for their zips, releasing their already hard or semi hard cocks. Still she does not see their faces, the members only recognisable to her by the difference in their cocks and cologne.

"Now my beautiful little whore, it's really time to earn your money."

Her mouth opens readily for the first, the pre-come swirling in her mouth like exotic mouthwash. Her tongue targeting the sensitive filament before sliding the full length of the shaft.

"Look at the slut she's loving it, let her take mine now," says another deeply authoritative voice,

Scarlet's head is jerked back releasing the cock, before it is forced onto a second cock, then a third. With gaps just long enough to catch her breath, her immediate life becomes a blur of pleasing these long hard cocks.

"Does your boyfriend know how much you like being used, slut?"

As bad as she would have felt to admit it, the thought of Matt watching had long since left her but now she did wonder. Wondered where he was watching from, wondered what he was making of her taking these five cocks at the same time.

The woman behind her now has fingers deep into Scarlet's pussy, working them in rhythm with the tongue still pleasuring her anus.

"Oh God no," Scarlett manages to call as her muscles first fold and then spasm around the slippery fingers as her second orgasm flows through her.

There is barely a moment in time before the fingers are replaced by a cock. Scarlet now so wet it barely meets resistance as the full length fills her.

Her hair jerked back slightly by the woman, who breathes into her ear.

"They will soon start to come. When they do you must not swallow, let the come drip from your mouth on to the altar below you."

Scarlet nods her understanding and hungrily lets her mouth work the waiting cocks. She decides to work each one in turn to climax. Her mouth folding tighter and tighter around the first shaft, her tongue flicking the filament. That fatal twitch and tightening, a loud animalistic grunt and the first load fills her mouth. The desire to let it slide down her throat nearly catches her unawares, but the woman sensing the position lowers her head by her hair till she dribbles it all onto the mirrored altar beneath her.

Her mouth is soon working again. The cock pumping her pussy faster and faster, harder and harder. She knows he is going to come, not inside she manages to whisper. The cock is withdrawn and pressed hard now against her wet and softened anus. The hot come leaping from the man's cock coating that forbidden hole.

As if synchronised the second load fills her mouth. Again her head is lowered and the come released on the altar, but as she looks at the puddled come, the altar becomes lit, turning what she thought was a mirrored surface into plain glass and she sees there below her lying on a shelf parallel with her, Matt, his face obscured and blurred by the come settled on the surface between them.

Their eyes lock and they share a brief but reassuring smile, before Scarlet's head is jerked back to please the third cock. The fifth enters her from behind. Her body now beautifully numbed by pleasure and in a constant state of mini orgasm, relaxes into a steady rhythm. Back on to the hard cock and forward onto the waiting shaft.

She pictures what Matt must be seeing as he watches her from below. Her small bare breasts juddering as her mouth takes this stranger's cock. She feels them close to coming. The man withdraws and joins his fellow member at her mouth. Their hands now pumping themselves to orgasms over her tongue.

With her mouth full Scarlet looks down to Matt, who she can tell is pumping himself. Slowly she drips the stranger's come onto the face of her watching boyfriend. His eyes, then groan tell her of his climax, as the final dribble hits the glass.

The light slowly dims and Scarlet can feel the members fading back into the shadows then leaving the room altogether. The woman helps Scarlet back onto her still trembling legs, gently kisses her lips before whispering a tender "goodnight."

She feels Matt's arms fold around her and they kiss softly neither uttering a word. He leads her to the changing room and within 35 minutes Tinto delivers Scarlet to her door.

"Do you mind if I sleep alone tonight," she whispers to Matt.

She feels bad, seeing the slightly hurt expression on his face but she needed time to think.

"No of course," he lies.

Matt is lying on his bed an hour later when a text arrives from Scarlet.

"You do know it's my birthday next."

Who said Crime Doesn't Pay?

Ben Cross sits at his desk nursing the tension in his temples, the cash flow projections for the following three months a swathe of red figures, now pushed to one side.

His phone rings

"It's Mr Engleman, Ben," says Louisa his receptionist come all round girl Friday.

"Put him through, Louisa."

"So how are things, Ben, tough I hear!"

And so Ben's conversation had started with Max Engleman, Hughes Brothers biggest client. A conversation that would change their relationship forever.

"Not so tough, Max, you shouldn't believe all that you hear," Ben had lied.

"I hope so, friend, as that's not what the market place is saying."

"No?"

"No I mean it's probably only gossip right," Max had patronisingly reassured. "It's just the rumour is if you don't secure the next big order I place you're fucked, finished, finito."

"And hopefully you put them right, Max," Ben responded, failing to hide his displeasure.

"No, Ben, I didn't."

That slight sneer that crawled like slime along the telephone line.

"It's true isn't it; if I don't place you're finished."

Ben's relationship with Max had been strained for some time. He was a ruthless bastard. Ben was in no doubt about that, but Ben had twenty-five staff and a lot of extended mouths to feed including his own family. It was time to come clean and just hope some deal could be struck. A deal that did not come at too high a price.

"It's not great to be honest, Max, but then it's not great for anyone right now."

"It puts a huge pressure on me too you know," chides Max," It may be my company here but I still have to satisfy my board of directors why I still use Hughes Brothers and not your competitors who are all cheaper."

Cheaper, because you screw them so tightly that their balls squeak, thinks Ben to himself.

"You know our products are much better, Max."

"Ben, that's not quite the point these days, eh? People don't care about quality anymore it's all about price. Price, price, price. Besides…"

"Besides…?"

"Besides, do you know what I get given by them as sweeteners Ben? Do you? Watches, jewellery, holidays, money, even a car once, but you – nothing."

Pending doom sinks like a heavy weight across Ben's already tired shoulders.

"But I like you, Ben."

Ben senses the wolf dressed as Grandma. I want to help."

"And?"

"And I have terms to put to you."

"What terms, Max?"

"My usual order, £100,000 will last you how long Ben, three months? We both know you have to last six months before your order from Hong Kong kicks in, then its happy days for you boy and adios Max, right?"

Ben's mind races, aware that somewhere, whether in his organisation or in the offices of his Accountants, he has been betrayed.

"Then, Ben, I may just be prepared to double my order. Yep £200,000. Utopia, eh?"

"And you'll do that for me?" Ben almost coldly asks, knowing the price of this proposal may be beyond him but even he not realising how high a price would be demanded.

"Of course," shouts Max almost over excitedly, almost over supportively. "All I want is one thing, one tiny thing."

"Which is?"

"Which is, Ben, I want your wife. I want to fuck your wife. Fuck her stupid. Fuck her so that every time you look at her, you and she both know what it took to save the company."

"You're a very sick man, Maximillian."

"Those are my terms, Ben, take them or leave them."

"But why her, Max? You've never even met her."

"I like power, Ben. I like control. I already own the fate of your company, now I want more."

"I need to think." Even Ben hadn't thought Max would sink to these terms, not to these depths.

"You have 24 hours to agree or I place the order elsewhere. Goodbye, Ben."

Ben, resigned to his fate, had lain next to his beautiful wife in a sleepless bath of torture whilst he had played and replayed every conceivable option, every possible outcome in his mind. Ideas percolated like bubbles teasing at his subconscious, but as his eyes finally closed he knew he would have to decide whether to speak with her in the morning.

The next afternoon he had phoned Max. Max who had left him in suspense as three times he had not taken Ben's call.

"You are a shit, Ben. I never thought you would agree, but a deals a deal. How did you get her to agree?"

"I haven't, not yet. She knows nothing of this. She is her own woman. But we will both meet you for dinner. I will give you every opportunity with her, Max."

"You don't get the order, Ben, unless I fuck her you do know that?"

"Yes I know that, Max, I know that, but I leave it in the hands of fate. Either you can persuade her or you can't. But Max...If you win and you don't place that contract I will kill you."

Ben had booked a table at an Italian Restaurant which he did not usually frequent but which had come highly recommended. He had booked to eat Al Fresco hoping that it would be a little more discreet with the forecast predicting cloudy weather.

Scarlet had sensed his nerves as he paced.

"Are you okay," she asked.

"Yes fine. Fine," he lied.

Scarlet snapped another breadstick.

"Ben, come sit. Please."

He had no sooner sat when the smart click of a uniform pair of shoes approached from behind.

"Ah, Max, this is my wife Scarlet. Scarlet, this is Max Engleman."

"Scarlett, it's a delight to meet you."

Ben looks beyond Max as if expecting the arrival of another.

"Ah I'm afraid my wife couldn't make it, not well I'm afraid. I'm sorry, I should have called to tell you."

"Never mind," said Ben, trying to make the position sound more spontaneous, "wish her better."

"Please don't worry, Scarlet, I'll try not to bore you with too much shop talk."

The conversation had flowed surprisingly freely, although Scarlet was finding a new respect for Ben's tact and diplomacy. Max was beautiful but clearly difficult. In fact, neither beautiful or difficult quite did Max justice. Scarlet tried to discretely take him in. Whilst superficially charming, the thin veneer could surprisingly quickly flip to arrogance and ignorance. The feeling that his alpha male pheromone was all it took to dictate the room. In one way a slow burning aphrodisiac, in another a behaviour so annoying it made Scarlet feel like stabbing him through the heart with her stiletto.

But physically he was a dish. One to be eaten hot or cold. Sharp blue suit with matching tie and crisp lapelled white shirt. Presented to perfection from the mint on his breath, the faint whiff of very expensive cologne and the fine coating of moisturiser just filling so slightly the fine lines that now etched his face and eyes as he smiled.

The starters came and went, the pick being the scallops chosen by Scarlet. Max not wasting the opportunity to take Scarlet's hand in his.

Ben's mobile suddenly lights and vibrates wildly across the table.

"I am so sorry both, please excuse me."

"Ben, do you have to? It's late," Scarlet scolds.

But it's too late. With a swish of pulled back chairs and waved hands, Ben leaves to take the call.

"Ah, in business," says Max, "time waits for no man, especially when every penny is a prisoner."

Scarlet glares at Ben for leaving her.

"I'm sorry, dear, am I boring you?"

"No I'm sorry, Max, it's just work always seems to come first these days. He is hardly ever home anymore and as for time together...Oh I'm sorry, Max, I shouldn't be telling you this."

"I'm glad you have. You should not be so hard on him, not with all of the troubles he has."

"Troubles? Ben has troubles? He has said nothing to me."

"Ah," Max takes a sip of his wine "Ben has kept you such a closely guarded secret, my dear."

Scarlet feels the blush rise within her.

"Why would Ben ever tell anyone about me?"

"Because, my dear, you are charming, funny, beautiful and very sexy."

"Max, are you flirting with me?"

"Flirting? Maybe."

"Max, what trouble is Ben in?"

Max rather noticeably checks the dining area to make sure he is not overheard.

"I should tell you straight? Exactly as it is?"

"Yes, Max, I want it straight, warts and all."

"Then I shall. His company is close to folding, I am the only one who can save it which is why I am dining here today."

"Folding? But he has said nothing to me."

"I am the only one who can save it. Save the company, save the jobs, save your lifestyle."

Scarlet's head sinks into her hands.

"Tell me more…"

"I can place an order that will keep the company trading for six months by which time an established order will come through. The company will be saved."

"So will you?" Scarlet's question hangs heavy in the air. "Will you save us, Max?"

"Scarlet, dear, business is a dog eat dog world. Sadly for you, Ben, his staff, I owe you nothing."

"So this is some macabre joke? You tell me that we are about to be ruined and refuse to save us, just what sort of man are you, Max?"

Scarlet almost regrets that she has found Max attractive at all. Instead considering now punching him so hard she can count his teeth as she picks them from the carpet.

"I didn't say I would not save you, Scarlet, I just want a reward for doing it – is that really too much to ask?"

"And the reward is, Max?"

"The reward is you of course."

The punching his teeth out option again springs close to Scarlet's temples, she going so far as to clench her fists.

"Don't be ridiculous."

"Scarlet," Max's voice adopts a cool emotionless ruthless tone "The deal is this. I get you. I get to fuck your brains out. I get to fuck you tonight, however and whenever. Do all I ask and you have my word I will place the order and save the company. Don't and this will be the last decent meal you have in a long time."

"Does Ben know about this?"

"My terms? No, dear, this is between you and me," the tone is one of sickly false comfort.

Scarlet exhales a deep breath.

"I need time," she pleads.

"You have fifteen minutes to decide. When Ben returns you will go to the ladies' room. If you accept my terms you will leave your knickers under the table. If they are not there by the time we finish our main courses, I shall take that as your final answer and make my excuses to leave."

At that very moment they hear Ben's returning footsteps.

"Sorry about that everyone. Everything okay?"

"Fine," snaps Scarlet, "excuse me."

And with that she picks up her bag and heads to the ladies' room. Her return is greeted both by Ben and Max but also by the arrival of their main courses.

"I'm sorry Max, but we will need to leave just as soon as we have finished, there is a problem at the office. An attempted break in, fortunately Louisa is dealing with the Police and the locks but I cannot leave her there all night."

Max stares at Scarlet as she picks only idly at her food. Their eyes lock. Max looks under the table. He smiles as the black lacy thong lies on the small piece of carpet between his and Scarlet's feet.

"Please, Ben, don't take the lovely Scarlet from me. We will finish our meal and I will make sure Scarlet is returned to you safely."

If Ben picked up on the nuance, his face betrayed nothing.

"Darling?" he asks of Scarlet.

"No its fine, Ben, you go, I'll make sure Max is looked after."

Just as soon as Ben has left, Max declines the offer of dessert or coffee and settles the bill. Within half an hour he and Scarlet are in a private booth in the cocktail bar within his hotel.

"You really will make me go through with this?" questions Scarlet as she gulps a little too quickly at her long island tea.

"Well unless you've decided to create twenty-five redundancies and join the dole queue, my dear, yes, I do."

"Just what sort of man are you, Max?"

"One who likes his pleasures dirty and perverse Scarlet, dirty and perverse. Another drink?"

Scarlet is drinking too quickly, but she needs to if she is to let her mind settle, now the reality of this is upon her.

With a barely imperceptible nod of his head Max hails the waiter.

"Same again please."

"I'm sorry, sir, I am just about to go off duty I will ask a colleague."

"No. I want you to do it," commands Max sliding a £50 note across the table.

"Yes, sir."

The beautiful boy, probably Brazilian is back at the table in less than five minutes.

"Your drinks, sir," he looks expectantly at the waiting note which Max duly slides across the table.

"How hung are you, boy?" Max asks.

The boy immediately shocked and unsure of his ground stammers.

"How hung, boy?"

The penny is dropping quicker than April rain.

"Well hung, sir."

"Want to earn £200 right now?"

"What is it you want me to do?" he hesitantly asks.

"My wife and I are swingers, we want you to join us."

"Max," Scarlet protests.

"The lady doesn't seem so sure," the waiter questions.

"It's a game, role play isn't it, dear?"

Max looks deep into Scarlet's eyes, a wordless reminder that she is to do whatever, whenever. Scarlett smiles at the waiter.

"Don't worry, its role play. You are beautiful and I like them well hung."

Max taps the back of her hand almost affectionately, almost as you would a dog who has faithfully retrieved a stick.

The moment is now upon her. They are simply waiting for the boy to change and join them at the booth. She looks to Max who half smiles, half smirks in return. The butterflies that have fluttered through her all afternoon are now smoothing into a disturbing want and desire. The helplessness of her situation, the sheer violation by Max of her wants and rights have now made her involuntarily leak her love juice onto her thighs. The alcohol now numbing the widest extreme of her fears. She is to be fucked not only by this beautiful boy but by this evil shit sitting by her side. This beautiful, ruthless, sexy, evil shit.

Scarlet barely remembers the walk to the lift or the small talk in the corridor leading to the room or the drinks poured by Max on their arrival there. No, the first she remembers is Max holding the back of her hair as he firmly guides her to her knees and says "you know what to do, darling, make him nice and hard for me."

Scarlet's mouth is level with the boy's crotch. Her palm instinctively presses itself firmly onto his zip. The shaft stirs into life, filling the material of his trousers.

"God you really are well hung," praises Max.

Scarlet, now fully in the moment, slowly unclips the trouser button and slides the zip to its lowest resting place before sliding her fingers into the boy's boxers and pulling both them and the trousers to his ankles.

His young cock not quite fully erect is already longer and thicker than anything she has ever seen. Now, needing no encouragement, her small hand folds as far around his shaft as she can and slowly stretches his foreskin forward and back over his huge purple helmet. She leans in so her tongue can delve into his come hole letting the salty gift tease her taste buds. She feels his tummy tense, then tense still further as her mouth folds around the knob. Max purrs as he sees Scarlet's mouth have to stretch wider than is comfortable to take it in.

"Hey, darling, don't forget your husband."

Max has lowered his own trousers and pants and is gently stroking himself hard. Scarlet sees his cock out of the corner of her vision but seems reluctant to leave the monster in her mouth. Her hair is pulled sharply back before Max roughly pulls her head onto his cock.

Scarlet can at least take in air comfortably as her tongue washes over his sensitive filament.

"Oh that is good, if only our friend Ben was here to watch. Don't you think?"

Scarlet lets the thought wash over her conscience. She has to.

Her mouth is pulled from one cock to the other. A blur of hotel room is all she sees before her mouth is filled by hard cock again, only knowing who she is pleasing by the size and girth.

Max is the first to break hold and lies back down on the bed with his hard cock far end. The boy leads her front on to the mattress so that she and Max get into a 69.

His expert tongue quickly delves between her pussy lips and laps at the juices freely flowing from her before it slides in and out of her cunt. She feels the boy nudging now at her pussy, Max's mouth moving to her clit.

Her long loud moan vibrates around the shaft of Max's cock as the monster knob stretches her so widely she fears it will tear. Breathing as if she is in labour, in and out, she manages to relax enough for the huge knob to press through her resistance. Filling her inch by inch until she feels it will pound her stomach, the boy is finally as far in as he can be. Opening Scarlet's anal cheeks wide to create just a little more room, he starts to slide in and out.

Scarlet is in sexual utopia. Being filled like never before, her mouth still valiantly swallowing Max's shaft, balls deep, his beautiful cologne still lingering in his shaped pubic hair.

She slowly feels confident enough to slide back and control the rhythm. As she slides forward to the tip of the beautiful Brazilian's knob she swallows deep on Max's shaft whilst he laps faster and faster on her juices. As she slides back on to the huge shaft her mouth rises to Max's now aching throbbing purple knob, while she hears Max's tongue lapping at the boy's balls.

The words used by Max in the bar "dirty and perverse," roll around Scarlet's mind, now abandoned from alliance of duty and obligation, as the waves grow deeper and deeper inside.

Her long whimpered cry fills the room dampened only by the cock still in her mouth. The cock that now twitches and erupts as Max's hot come fills her mouth then disappears down the back of her throat.

The boy still hard slides out of her enabling her to slump on the bed desperate to catch her breath and let the throbbing subside.

As she slumps, her anus smothers Max's mouth. She feels his hot wet breath tease it, feels his breathing slow and that breathing then replaced with the tiny tip of a tongue sending shivers through her.

Through her slightly blurred vision she sees the beautiful boy stroking himself to retain that iron hard shaft. With the tongue now trying to break through her resistant anal muscle, Scarlet lazily strokes at Max's balls surprised to feel his cock already turning hard.

With time no bar, the tension builds. Max's tongue now through the muscle filling the passage beyond with his hot saliva. His shaft now fully hard under Scarlet's pumping hand.

The boy lifts Scarlet gently. Max slides into a sitting position and the boy lowers Scarlet till her lubricated anus is now pressing against Max's reinvigorated cock. Gently her anus lets Max in till she sinks onto his full shaft, the initial sharp pain settling into a heavy ache. Max stretches Scarlet's legs wide then lets his fingers fold around her hard nipples and pulls her close.

The boy suddenly kneels before her rubbing his huge knob against her pussy, tightened by her anus being stretched.

"No, No, I won't be able to take it – please" she begs. It's as if the boy doesn't hear a word. Slowly, just as before, his huge cock fills her. The two cocks now within her, separated only by a thin membrane between pussy and arse.

Taking it in turns to fuck her. As the boy stops and holds himself inside, Max pumps hard and deep into her anus. As Max holds still inside, the boy slides his huge length, in and out.

Scarlet is fucked like a rag doll as her body, softened by the exertion, is used for their pleasure. A series of small orgasms evolves into one long painful but pleasurable climax.

She now barely notices as the boy withdraws and holding his knob at the entrance to her mouth pumps hard. It is only as Max deposits his come deep inside her anus and stills that the boy erupts, his come spurting into her mouth and over her face and neck for as long as his moan fills the air.

The boy will shortly dress and leave £200 richer and with his balls empty and aching nicely in his jeans, but Max has not yet finished. That is, finished using Scarlet as he wants. It is only in the early hours that they finally fall into a deep slumber in a pile of contorted limbs.

The whole situation has left Scarlet physically and mentally exhausted. The feeling that her own deviance has betrayed her. A sense of shame she has enjoyed it all so much, so much that she even now feels the need to slide her hands beneath the sheet and gently stroke her abused clit.

She has woken late. Max has left. The shit that he is, he has not paid for the room, Scarlet smiles. "If he doesn't place the order, I will kill the fucker myself" she says out loud to herself.

She buys coffee then drives in a sombre mood to the office to face Ben. As she enters his office, he is sitting behind his desk, eyes closed, clearly reflecting on the events of the last seventy-two hours.

"I did it, I did what you wanted, Ben." Her voice quiet, hesitant. He looks at her differently than he has ever done before, his mind unreadable.

"I know, he placed the order. He's a fucker but strangely good to his word."

Scarlet smiles, but he is too distant to notice the gesture instead reaching into his drawer and pulling out the company cheque book.

You see there is one part to this story I have kept from you. One important part. Let us go back to Ben's sleepless night, the night after Max had put forward his terms, the night where the idea had fermented in his mind.

This is what had happened…

Scarlet felt sick. Felt sick as she had listened in silence as Ben had prowled around her, slowly and methodically producing evidence of her wrong doing. Her heart raced and the nausea rose within her.

£10,000 was missing from various Bank accounts. £500 here, £750 there and in each case the money had been drawn on a form issued in another name but clearly signed by her. Of course she knew she had signed the forms and had the money. She had protested her innocence long and determinedly, but even she had to admit the evidence was overwhelmingly against her.

"But aside from these forms you have no evidence I received any of this money."

"No?" Ben said coolly, "open your bag."

"What?" Scarlet had said, failing to disguise the anxiety that was washing through her.

"Your bag, Scarlet."

Scarlet opened her handbag.

"What am I supposed to be looking for exactly?"

"You don't know?" His voice dripped with a vaguely disguised cruelty.

"No of course I don't."

"There's not a brown envelope in there then?"

Scarlet felt the blood rush through her temples. There was as she knew, a brown envelope. She pulled out the contents, £500 in cash.

"But I've never seen this before."

Ben starts to prowl.

"This morning a false invoice was submitted with a cheque request slip to accounts, approved and signed by you, but in the name of Derek Young."

Ben passes her the slip. The signature a good likeness, but when compared to Derek Young's own signature, an obvious forgery.

"Accounts did of course tell me of their concerns. I authorised the payment. The envelope was left in Derek's tray but taken from there by you."

"But I...," started Scarlet.

"But what, Scarlet? We have the form, the signature and the money." Ben left the pause hanging heavy in the air. "Scarlett you have been one of the most trusted of employees here. We have known each other for years. You know the difficulties we have. This is a massive breach of trust."

Scarlet studies Ben's face. His normally sparkling eyes and broad, almost cute smile, was now cool and distant.

"I am afraid, Scarlet, I will need to bring in the Police. Well that is unless..."

And that is when Ben had told Scarlet of the position of the Company, how close it was to folding and of Max's terms.

"So let me get this straight," Scarlet speaks slowly hoping her brain will catch up with the words now coming from her mouth. "You expect me to pretend to be your wife and fuck the customer?"

"No, Scarlet, I expect you to go to jail for theft. I am simply offering you the chance to avoid that unfortunate outcome and the chance to redeem yourself, to save the jobs of your colleagues and the Company."

"And to be given another £5,000 if I do it right?"

Scarlet is savvy, her quick mind detecting that the emphasis of the situation has changed; she now knows Ben needs her.

"£3,000," counter offers Ben.

"£5,000. Whatever he is offering I am worth every penny."

"You do whatever he wants, however he wants. You do it as my wife. If he signs the order I forget your indiscretions and you get £5,000. If you don't…"

The sentence is never finished.

So now, good to his, word Ben writes out the cheque to Scarlet for £5,000. The pair stare at each other with a new respect that can only arise from the shared experience.

Their fingers fold into each other's then with a smile of acknowledgement that the adventure has passed, Scarlet rises to leave. Ben's landline rings. He lets it ring three times before saying to Scarlet.

"Stay. Listen."

He presses the loudspeaker, it is Max. A very angry Max.

"You fucker, you absolute fucker."

"Thank you for your order, Max, you know how important it is to us."

"Don't give me that. I'll fucking kill you."

Ben cuts off the call, sinks back in to his chair and smiles.

"Oh, he has found out about me?" Scarlet guesses.

"No, Scarlet, I could not risk negating the deal. No I sent him this…"

Ben hands her his phone. The screen reveals a slightly blurred freeze frame but when Scarlet touches the screen there is a video. A video of a beautiful brunette, legs draped tight around Ben's toned back.

"Fuck me, fuck me Ben," the woman cries out.

"Who, who is she?" Scarlet asks.

"Meet Max's wife, the beautiful Mrs Engleman. She gets very lonely with Max spending so much time away from home."

Scarlet laughs to herself as she leaves, then laughs even more as she reaches into her handbag and pulls out the very expensive pen she has just pinched from Ben's desk, the one with which he has just written out the cheque now clutched tightly in her hand.

The Final Dare

Just how far would you go?

The game of dare and forfeit had reached its climax. Over the preceding six months the initially playful dares had evolved to an ever escalating level which had incurred at least two informal cautions from passing Police patrol cars. But now the final dare and it has fallen to you on the toss of a coin. Of course you could always say NO at any point but we both knew you wouldn't, not even now we have just parked in the busy supermarket car park. I step out into the car park, secure a trolley and wait. Your bare ankle dressed in a beautiful closed red five-inch heel steps from the passenger side. The moment is caught in the perfect pause. There are two guys talking. One doing his recycling, the other a hand car washer. They see the moment and stop. Their faces turn to expressions of sheer lust as your long bare leg stretches from the car only to be quickly covered by your only other item of clothing – a matching pvc mac. You straighten the mac, smile enigmatically at your appreciative audience, shake your hair from your eyes and walk to me. I see the recycling guy shake his head in jealous disbelief as I hand cuff your proffered hands to the pushing rail of the trolley.

The plan is that you must buy three items I have chosen for you then I will meet you at the checkout to pay. The thing is, of course, that you will have to ask complete strangers to help you get the items from the shelf.

I stand a safe distance away and watch in erotic admiration as you drift along the aisles with apparent total disregard to the attention you are receiving. The reality is of course very different. The throb in your temples is pulsing so fast you feel your head will explode. With every second that passes you are waiting for the hand of the security guard to be placed firmly on your shoulder or for someone to unveil you. The adrenalin runs through your body every time you catch someone stop and watch as your long bare leg stretches from the mac or when someone sees your cuffed wrists and gives you a knowing smile or soft wink.

The first items are two cheap ties.

You drift to the men's section. The fear gradually transforming into a forbidden thrill and a tingling soreness as the mac rubs against your hard nipples. You see me at the end of the aisle watching you. This will be the most difficult part, asking a stranger to help. A procession of unsuitable people pass you and you start to despair. You look to me for help but I just smile coolly.

"You look like you could do with a hand," says the deep voice from behind you. You turn and jump. "I've been watching you," he says "although to be fair so has every other man with a cock in this shop."

Your eyes are lured into his. Deep brown like melting maltesers; his perhaps over assured smile, cute but slightly unsettling.

"I am feeling a little restrained today," you say in a confident voice which betrays the shuddering anticipation now rolling through your mind. "I need two ties," you continue. "Could you please?"

"Any ties in particular?"

Oh that deep voice. Just a hint of husk and lust.

"Just cheap. I have my instructions" you say. He looks around calmly but he doesn't see me. He picks up two.

"Hideous but cheap," he says.

"Hideous but cheap are perfect," you say.

A smile passes between you.

"Anything else I can help with he asks?"

"Two more items."

A tear of love juice escapes you as the word condoms escapes your mouth. "Oh and a half bottle of champagne" you virtually whisper.

"Let's do the champagne first," he says helping guide you to the chiller at the bottom of the wine aisle. He opens the fridge.

"Any one in particular," he asks as he opens the door and rolls his palm across the settled ice.

"The shop brand will be fine," you say.

Without a word of warning you feel his chilled hand slip between your buttons onto your tummy. The underlying muscles tightening as you feel his fingertips drift so very softly to the tip of your defenceless bare vulnerable pussy lips. Your eyes are locked and you feel a very gentle whimper of want escape your lips. You are screened from everyone bar me. Our eyes exchange messages.

"I am okay" yours say "I want this to continue."

"I am told this one is much nicer," he says pulling a half bottle with an alternative brand from the chiller and placing it in your trolley. "So condoms is it?" he smiles. "You have an eclectic shopping list."

"It's not my list," you say, some calm returning. "Like I say I have my instructions."

The aisle containing the condoms is empty. He holds the trolley still as he virtually breathes into your ear the qualities of each and every rubber and lubricant. You feel that wave of ache and pleasure virtually sucking on your clit as his deep voice tells you how one in particular is made for deep, hard, rough, defenceless fucks. You gasp long and breathlessly as his hand again slips through your buttons and pinches your right nipple. You can virtually feel his minty breath on your tongue as if his teeth are going to tug on your bottom lip. Our eyes meet again. I go to step towards you to end this, but your eyes flash "I want this".

"So which one do I get he says?"

"Sometimes only the hard defenceless fuck will do," your broken voice stammers in response.

"Good. My favourite."

You both head towards the checkout. This is where it was planned I would uncuff you and pay, but something tells me to hold back. You guide the trolley to the checkout. The stranger chats amiably to the young checkout boy who suddenly notices the cuffs and allows his eyes to wander over your defenceless body. The look of sheer desire in the young man's face both scares and excites you. Of course you are older but it is clear that if there was one wish he could have, it would be you. The stranger pays and guides you and the trolley from the shop.

"I should shop with you more often," the stranger jokes. "He only charged you for the champagne and one tie."

You suddenly realise the dynamic of the situation has changed. The stranger guides you beyond our car in the principle carpark through to the corner of the over flow carpark. Here the trees are over grown slightly and there is a rarely used bay for returning trolleys. You know I will follow. You are standing out facing the carpark. You see me roughly 20 metres in front of you crouched between two parked cars. Our eyes lock again – your eyes sparkle with lust.

This is further than we have ever been with another person. My stomach is in knots; watching that lust in your eyes. Part of my soul is crying; its tears, though, in the form of pre come from my come hole. We have always agreed the other could play. We just never have and now you are on the verge. I want to stop this. I want him to fuck your brains out.

The stranger takes the ties and condoms from the trolley. You feel him guide your ankles apart. You feel him tie one end of the first tie around your right ankle and the other to the post of the bay. Then the left with the second tie. He reaches around to your defenceless front and very slowly undoes your buttons. Pulling your coat back over your shoulder. Your entire body is now bared to anyone who may pass. You hear him rip open the packaging. His swollen knob now pressing against your soaking entrance.

"Do you want me to fuck you, bitch?" He provokes in your ear. "Do you want my cock or shall I just leave you tied up so any old man can have his way with you?"

"No fuck me," you hear yourself say. "Please. just you. Fuck me, fuck me."

Just as your words escape you, you feel his cock tease your pussy then slide the full length deep inside you.

Your legs buckle and it is only the ties around your ankles that keep you upright. His cock glistening with your musky sticky juices starts to slide in and out. Your rhythm and pleasure entirely in his gift. I see the serene pleasure in your eyes. Your bare breasts leaping from your torso as he starts to fuck you harder and faster. Even from my distance I hear a deep growl drift from your mouth across the car park. Your head jerks back as his hand grabs your hair. I can see you are both close to orgasm. He now holds your hair in one hand and your breast tight in the other as he pounds you with one last effort. I hear your groans as the deep intense waves of pleasure and pain grind, tease and fuck their way through your tummy, pussy and thighs. The stranger whips off his condom and you feel his hot come land on the back of your thighs. He unties your ankles then whispers softly in your ear.

"Thank you."

Your eyes are still shut as I arrive to untie you.

"Oh my God," you gently whisper under your breath as the final waves of your orgasm kiss the soft pads of the bottom of your toes.

The stranger has gone. I remove the cuffs and hold you in my strong arms till your legs no longer shake.

"Oh my God," you say again as you feel the strangers come drip slowly along your thighs and drop in small puddles by the side of your fuck me heels.

I pull out the champagne and pop the cork. You take the first swig.

"To the best ever dare," you say. Just how did you set that up, who was he?"

"Darling, I didn't. I really have no idea."

"Oh," you say.

We both swig another sip from the bottle and let the enormity of what has just happened settle. And then you smile, that smile that has caused so much mischief.

"Does this really have to be the final dare?" you ask letting me have that soft, slow, naughty wink.

The Master of the House

"Tonight, Scarlet, the Master has asked that you attend upon him."

The news is broken to her with a clipped cruelty by Mrs Montgomery, the senior housekeeper, as the staff eat their early evening meal.

The news is greeted with giggles by two of the youngest chambermaids and with a shiver down the spine by Scarlet.

Daisy who is normally charged with the task has not been seen all day.

Scarlet has never met her employer notwithstanding she has been in his employ as junior governess to his orphaned youngest child for three months.

In fact, she has come no closer to meeting him than seeing the chamber maids polishing the big brass plaque bearing his name on the big oak door to his grand but imposing residence in the east end of London.

"Lord Black appointments by written request only."

Black is elusive, rarely seen by anyone anywhere. So far as she is aware only Mrs Montgomery and Daisy within the house have ever met him.

From her conversations with other junior governesses in the park his reputation is just as mysterious out of the house as it is within.

Rumours abound how he came by his wealth, there being few suggestions that it was by fair means.

"Mrs Montgomery," Scarlet hesitatingly begins.

"Yes Scarlet?"

"Just what are my duties in attending upon the Master?"

The giggles from the same two junior chambermaids are cut short with a venomous glare from Mrs Montgomery.

"Scarlet, you simply do as the Master commands."

Scarlet is due to attend upon him at 7.30, an hour after her charge has been put to bed. She feels a trembling foreboding run like a ghost through every fibre. A temptation to run. "Run Scarlet," – the whispers run with the rhythm of a steam train through her mind.

But Scarlet knows that for the poor, in the east end of London, in Victorian times life is tough, with positions of privilege few and far between.

She knocks gently at the bedchamber door.

"Come," the responding voice, a deep soft Celtic brogue.

Scarlet tentatively enters the huge room. The room lit by a vast array of different sized candles.

It takes some time for Scarlet's eyes to adjust to the mix of glaring bright lights and deep impenetrable shadows.

Her eyes take in the wood panelled walls and roaring log fire before settling on the four-poster bed with the opulent black silk sheets adorned with manacles, cuffs and chains. Before the bed is a bath filled deeply with steaming perfumed water.

The smell of patchouli mixed with the deep, peaty, smoking smell of the fire drifts into her senses.

Scarlet searches the room for her Master, but it is only when he strikes a match to light his cigar that she sees him, oh so briefly. A striking, but battle-hardened face. Now Scarlet knows where he is, she realises he is sitting, sitting and watching her, the perfumed smoke from his cigar curling towards her.

"Sir?" Scarlet whispers her voice almost cracking.

From behind her the door opens and a stiff walking Daisy enters. With only a fleeting exchange of eye contact, she stands behind Scarlet and slowly starts to unclip her dress.

"Daisy," Scarlet scolds as she turns sharply.

"She is following my orders," the Celtic brogue cuts through the moment.

"If you would prefer her to disobey my wishes that is of course your entitlement Miss Kiss. You will of course let Mrs Montgomery know the name of your new employer won't you?"

The threat confirms the darkest of Scarlet's fears and suspicions "Run Scarlet," the steam engine churns its warning along the tracks inside her head. But Scarlet is a realist. With her limited savings she could be in the workhouse within the month. Besides there is something about the situation that has created a want within her, a feeling of vulnerability, of helplessness. A desire to experience this man.

As if allowing her just enough time to reconcile her thoughts he provokes.

"Well, Scarlet?"

Scarlet stands proud, her decision made. Her eyes sparkle like precious stones as Daisy removes her outer dress then leads her closer to her Master.

One by one the whale bone clips are released until the weight of the corset is in Daisy's gift. Slowly she allows it to lower then fall to the floor. Scarlet's breathing betrays her torment. Her young breasts stand proud, her nipples aching under his gaze, as if being held in a heavy pinch.

She feels Daisy's fingers reach inside her bloomers and slowly, so slowly, they are lowered over her hips until she stands bare just six feet before him. Her hands move to cover her modesty.

"No, Scarlet," his soft voice commands.

He says nothing more. As if by unspoken command Daisy pulls a lever and two wrist cuffs on long leather leads are lowered from the ceiling. With a mixture of horror and desire running through her Scarlet submits to Daisy's control and is manacled in place. Her bareness complete and exposed.

Scarlet does not expect what happens next. She screams as the first swoosh fills the air and the flogger leaves its first mark across her shoulders. The second marks her thighs and the third, the back of her calf. The sting has barely had time to turn to that deep glowing heat before the fourth and fifth blows send wheals across her bottom cheeks. She slowly loses count and slumps a little under the weight of the following blows. And then the pause. She hears Daisy panting just a little from the exertion. The stings slowly turn to heat then a deep throbbing. Scarlet's eyes still sparkle defiantly, her body aglow.

The throbbing now changing into an involuntary pleasure. Knowing it's for him, for his pleasure, feeling his eyes upon her. Her pussy spasms as a deep orgasm burns through her thighs. It is the sound of her own whimper that brings her back to real time.

Daisy releases her wrists and holds Scarlet until she feels her take her own weight.

She leads her slowly to the bath and holds her hand as she gingerly sinks into its fragranced heat.

Her cry is audible as the hot water floods her wounds.

"Just breathe deeply and slowly," Daisy advises. She holds Scarlet's hand tightly just before she steps back towards the fire.

Scarlet focusses on the bath water. The small tide created by her entry making the rose petals and lavender leaves swirl in small circles.

Three gold rings drift between the petals, their coating slowly melting and releasing the patchouli in little steam vapours into the room.

The stings gradually become a pleasure, a deep painful pleasure.

She watches as Daisy pulls her simple white smock over her head leaving herself bare to them both. More full figured than Scarlet with big oval breasts housing full pink nearly red hard nipples, wide hips perfectly framing a small blond bush of intimate hair. As beautiful as she is, it is the weals and deeper scars that criss-cross her breasts and tummy, thighs and upper arms that draw Scarlet's eyes, that make her head spin. Knowing she has been with him. That he has used her. Scarlet knows it is a union she wishes to join. How she hopes her own wheals excite him as much as Daisy's excite her.

Daisy sinks to her knees by the side of the bath and using a golden oil poured into her hand slowly starts to wash Scarlet's neck and shoulders, before cupping hot water in her hand and slowly rinsing the skin free of the formed bubbles.

Scarlet's eyes lock with Daisy's as her fingers now lather the oil into Scarlet's breasts, gently gliding the tips of her fingers over the firm mounds before settling on and circling her stiff nipples.

Scarlet cannot disguise her lust from Daisy's gaze. Again the cupped hand rinses the foam away, the hot water teasing her throbbing stems.

Daisy's hand now drifts along Scarlet's tummy, then along the outside of her thighs to her knee and then from the knee along the inside of her thigh until Scarlet feels it settle on the top of her guarding pussy lips. Daisy very slowly glides her finger nails along Scarlet's pussy lips. Her touch so light but bringing almost unbearable pleasure. Simultaneously Daisy lowers her mouth onto Scarlet's nipple and lets her fingers drift through her pussy lips and quickly onto her already stiff clit. Her fingers circle Scarlet's clit again so gently, so lightly. The exquisite tingles contrast with the ache of Daisy's mouth sucking hard on her nipple as if trying to draw milk.

Scarlet stares into the shadows housing her Master. Knowing he is watching her. Watching her now be pleasured. The thought of Daisy's wheals and scars vie for attention with the thought of his hard cock inside her.

The pictures becoming more vivid and perverse as Daisy's expert fingers bring her closer and closer to her orgasm.

Her cry almost melodic in its feminine beauty, is aimed at him as her clit unable to escape Daisy's fingers, she twitches and bucks as the orgasm shudders through her. The deep heat floods her loins and thighs, her breathing short and sharp. Colours flashing through her now closed eyes.

She barely focusses on the naked Daisy retiring to the fire and sliding her smock back over her head and then him, the Master leaving his darkened theatre and now walking towards her.

Still in the aftershocks of her orgasm, she sees him remove his shirt before her. His strong muscled shoulders and tight pecs themselves dressed in aged scars, deep and permanent. He reaches into the bath and lifts her clear, his muscles making her feel weightless. He takes the towel offered by Daisy and without a word pulls Scarlet's head to his chest and softly pats her dry.

"You have done well, Scarlet, let me tend to your wounds."

He leads her the short distance to the bed and lays her front down on the silken sheets. She senses him unbuttoning his own trousers then hears him slide them to the floor. He straddles her, his thighs either side of her bottom cheeks. His long hard cock resting in her crack.

Scarlet feels his warm breath on her back then his tongue gentle gliding along the length of her deepest wound. The sting is delicious. He kisses inch by inch until he reaches the next wound where again his tongue glides along its full length. Her fingers grip at the silk then wind it into her hands as his tongue finally stops at the top of her bottom cheeks.

She listens as he reaches for a bottle then smells the perfumed balm he pours it into his hands. The cool oil spread gently over her back by his gentle touch. The pain and heat extinguished almost on contact.

The gentle touch that turns into a firmer knead of her bottom cheeks. And then her hips raised so she is on all fours. His oiled fingers circling her soaking wet entrance resisting her attempts to edge back so they have to enter her.

"Please Master."

The first oiled finger enters almost without resistance and is shortly joined by a second. Scarlet's muscles grip around them as the fingers slide deep. It is the third finger that stretches her just a little. Scarlet cannot help but let her groan escape. A deep purring groan. The fourth finger stretches her like she never has stretched before. The Master's fingers entirely filling her cavity.

He waits until her muscles relax before slowly his fingers start to glide in and out. A deep moan escapes Scarlet every time the fingers stretch her pussy and fill her entirely. As the fingers slowly increase their speed the moan becomes a constant hum filling the room. In and out. Touching every side of her cavern. The strong fingers massaging and pounding her G spot in equal measure. The fluid she has never felt before suddenly splashes through her and over his fingers before erupting from her pussy in three large pulsating squirts. Her body is no longer her own but a vehicle of pleasure. Her brain no longer reasoning or rationalising just letting the pleasure bring an aching abandoned numbness.

She doesn't even realise he has retired from her and left the room. It is Daisy who covers her in silken sheets then slides in beside her and holds her close.

"The Master is very pleased with you, Scarlet. You are to attend upon him again tomorrow."

The words barely seep into Scarlet's exhausted body and mind before she drifts into a deep aroused sleep.

The Beach

The holiday had proved to be the disaster Scarlet had predicted. Stella and Jen had fallen out when Rachael had unfortunately let slip that Stella had slept with Jen's ex Chris. The fur and hair flew and they had each departed under their own steam back to London. Rachael had then been buried in a wave of DVD's, chardonnay and Marlbrough silk cut cigarettes till her extra low cut top had caught the eye of one of the local lifeguards. That had been four days ago and Scarlet had not seen her since.

So this left Scarlet

They had together rented a house in the wilds of Cornwall for three weeks and there was still one and a bit to go. Scarlet had thought about returning to London herself but as a trainee teacher money was tight and the cottage was fully paid for.

She had spent the next three days doing the usual tourist's sights like the Eden project and Land's End and had feasted on the local seafood till she thought mussels would reappear through her nose if she ate just one more. Then as if a big sigh had flooded through her, she had started to relax.

She had taken to walking down the path cut into the cliff face to spend the evening on the small sheltered beach below. It had taken her two days to realise that no one else ever came here. This was now Scarlet's secret cove.

The routine was set. She would bring a salad together with a bottle of Cotes de Rhone, her radio and of course the holiday book. She would read for a while then take a dip in the cool refreshing sea before eating her tea and tucking into the wine and another 50 pages.

Tonight had started no differently. She had started to read and sipped her way through her first glass of red. She looked out to the sea and let the evening sun now catch her slightly freckled, sun kissed nose.

Time for a swim she had said to herself...

A sense of mischief passed through her. She checked she was alone, then released her bikini top allowing her cute pert breasts to sway forward. Then she slipped her panties from her toned creamy behind and slipped gently into the sea. She waded till the waves slapped across her newly shaven pussy lips sending a tingle through her before sliding into the waves. The cool water prickled across her body. As her air ran short she surfaced and gasped to fill her lungs. She was at least 20 yards now from shore. She sleeked her hair back and looked down at her creamy white breasts surrounded by tanned skin. The cool water made her beautiful brown nipples stand long and hard from the supporting mound. She tweaked her left nipple and gasped at the severity of her own torture before the pleasant pain flooded through her

She swam a while longer before breaststroking to shore. The evening was warm and balmy and she knew her skin would soon dry without the need for a towel. She poured a second glass of wine and tucked into her book lying on her towel and her still naked tummy. As in the previous evenings her eyes had soon started to weigh heavy and she let her head rest on the sand before slipping into an aroused sleep in which she had become a beautiful but depraved mermaid.

The crack woke her with a jolt. She had been asleep for some time and the evening was now showing the tell-tale signs of turning to night. She turned her head to the right. A fire fed with driftwood was glowing no more than ten feet from her.

"Oh shit," she thought.

Still lying to hide her modesty Scarlet did her best to check the beach. No one! So who lit the fire?

She pulled the towel around her and sat up. A rucksack lying close to the fire was her only clue. She headed towards it and started to peer in without disturbing the buckles.

"I see you found my secret cove then," Came a male voice

Scarlet looked along the beach and then to the cliffs in search of the voice

"I'm here."

The man called from the sea where he had been swimming. Scarlet's heart pounded. He was gorgeous. His eyes sparkled and his white teeth shone from a cute happy smile. He sleeked the water from his shaven head and started to rise from the water. His shoulders curved and wove into his toned biceps and triceps. His chest rounded and toned gave way to a flat tanned stomach. He wore short boxers and Scarlet noticed the semi erect shaft of his cock outlined against the material.

"Hi I'm Ben...So what do you think of my secret cove?"

"Your secret cove? I think you'll find it's mine," smiled Scarlet in response.

"Um, well, I've been coming here most days since I was 12 so I think you'll find it's mine, but I'll share."

Ben headed to the fire and shook the droplets from his toned body into the fire making it snap and crackle. He pulled his own wine from a cooler and offered a top up to Scarlet which she accepted.

"So tell me about you," he said, "and how you came to be naked on my beach?" asked with a teasing smile.

The pair talked for the best part of an hour. Scarlet told of the debacles which had hit the holiday to date and Ben in turn had told her of his life. The good news was that he was single and for good measure seemed laid back and fun. Scarlet felt the wine reach her toes and felt the tell-tale signs of her inhibitions slipping.

"You're very beautiful," said Ben suddenly

"Now I know you've drunk too much wine," Scarlet responded

I mean it and with that Ben leant across to kiss her.

Scarlet felt her lips drawn to his like a moth to a flame and started to lean towards him before she regained her composure and pulled back.

Laughing she put her fingers to his lips.

"Oh no I'm a good girl," she started to say

But Ben wasn't to be put off. He took the tip of Scarlet's finger into his mouth. The cool wine within his mouth flooded over the finger before his warm rough tongue massaged the tip. Ben continued the finger fuck by closing his lips tightly around the finger and taking its length in him.

The moment was so intimate under the stars and with the sand soft beneath her toes Scarlet felt her pussy ache.

"Naughty!" was all she could say but even then her voice was deep and distracted offering Ben every incentive to continue.

He withdrew her finger and kissed the tip gently

"I have a magic place where I have never ever taken anybody. Would you trust me enough to come with me?"

Scarlet smiled, "Yes I trust you. God knows why though."

Ben picked up his rucksack and headed for the water.

Stay here I'll be back for you in a short while

He glided into the sea holding the rucksack above his head to ensure it did not get wet. He soon disappeared from view as the dusky evening swallowed him.

After a few minutes the doubts started surfacing in Scarlet's head. This was potty. She had only just met this man and here she was contemplating swimming with him out into the black sea. She wrapped the towel tighter around her and rose to leave.

"Hey where are you going?" called Ben returning to the beach

"Uh I'm not sure this is such a good idea," said Scarlet.

Ben walked up the beach and took Scarlet's hands.

"Trust me," he said, "I know you don't know me but I promise you will be glad you came. I promise."

He guided her to the sea then standing behind her he loosened her towel so it slipped to the floor. She heard him slide off his shorts.

"Don't be shy," he smiled.

The moon was starting to reflect off the sea as Ben dived in. Conscious of her nudity Scarlet followed. Ben led her away from her usual swimming route. They swam beyond the rocks then walked through a small warm pool before sliding back into the deeper sea. They did not need to swim much further before they reached a small cluster of rocks that rose from the sea. Scarlet wondered how she had not seen them before but then realised they could not be seen as they were tucked away from the mainland. As they neared she noticed that the rocks were open to form a small sheltered pool. A glow came from inside. They swam in and she gasped.

The pool had been a cave with sides as high as 20 feet. The roof had fallen in many years before and the stars shone brightly in the sky above. The rocks which had fallen from the roof had formed 3 steps that opened before her like an altar. Each step had a thick covering of sand and was lined with candles that Ben had lit and which glowed and reflected on the walls giving it the look of an ancient Cathedral.

"Wow," was all she could say

"Don't worry," said Ben "The water is quite shallow here you can put your foot down."

Scarlet turned to Ben. He looked even more handsome in the candlelight

"Ouch!" Scarlet stubbed her toe.

Ben laughed.

"Thanks," said Scarlet keeping her naked chest below water level.

"Come here," said Ben

As she did so he lifted her in one easy movement onto the first step

Scarlet tried to cover her hard nipples from view.

"Hey, honey," he said. "You are gorgeous, there's no need to hide."

He lifted her foot and saw the graze. He kissed it gently, then took the toe into his mouth. Scarlet had never had her toe sucked before, but rather than the ticklish sensation she had been expecting, the tingles ran along her calves. The sight of this gorgeous man in the magical pool was starting to make her horny. Very horny. She watched entranced as the expert tongue worked along her calves and inner thigh. She groaned. Ben kissed her tummy and as if by an unspoken instruction she lay back to receive him.

Ben kissed her outer lips gently. Scarlet's already swelling clit peaked through and was greeted by a long slow lick. She shivered in anticipation. Ben opened her hood and she felt his tongue tease her entrance before it delved inside. Ben moaned as Scarlet's sweet sticky love juice hit his taste buds. His tongue was long and surprisingly hard. It seemed to fill her hot little hole. In and out like a lithe wet cock, the tongue teased and probed. His tongue coated with her musky love juice, Ben takes her clit in his mouth and teases it gently with a tiny bite. Scarlet arches her back on the blanket of sand and looks to the sky. The stars twinkle and the light-headedness of her building orgasm makes her feel that she could fly, feeling like slut Wendy to this gorgeous Peter Pan.

"Oh God, I'm coming. I'm coming," Scarlet surprises herself with the speed and intensity of her orgasm. Her loud moans echo around the stone walls.

Wave after intense wave flowing through her, her clit and pussy aching and tingling with pleasure.

Slowly the waves subside and her breathing softens.

She smiles coyly at Ben. "Oh I'm so sorry."

He says nothing, smiles then kisses her softly. Long and slow. His tongue dancing with Scarlet's. The sweetness of the wine and her love juice still on his breath. He slides her back into the pool so she is standing before him. She reaches below the surface. His cock is hard lean and long. They kiss again but this time she gently starts to roll his foreskin over his swollen knob and back again. He lifts her so each of her legs grip his hips under the water, then enters her.

He rocks her gently so he can control how much of his cock enters her with each thrust. They kiss again.

"Oh, baby," he murmurs.

She feels her waves building for a second time. This time less dynamic, more like a deep aching throb. Ben groaning quietly under his breath.

Harder and faster his shaft fills her.

"Stop," she said "stop."

He looks quizzically as he releases her. She mounts the steps so she faces him. He steps onto the first step. His swollen purple knob in line with her mouth. She takes him in hungrily and soon feels comfortable taking in his full length. In and out then teasing his filament and come hole.

She feels the betrayal of his pending climax and releases him, then lays back and softly but firmly commands.

"Stand over me. I want to see you come."

Ben stands over Scarlet one leg either side of her hips. He grabs his cock firmly and starts to pump. Hard and fast like a piston. Scarlet looks up dreamily. The silhouette of Ben's muscular frame stands out against the stars. His wanking shadow projected onto each wall.

Scarlet reaches between her legs pinches her tender clit then starts to massage it, faster and faster in time with Ben

"Let's come together, baby, please," she says in a deep but soft voice... "Please together."

Ben is close. His balls are tightening just above Scarlet's bare petite chest the pale mounds like a target to his airborne assault. Then he comes. His salty come leaping like lava from his body landing on her breasts and hard brown nipples.

The view takes Scarlet to orgasm and she writhes and convulses with pleasure as her fingers tease her clit.

Ben collapses onto Scarlet and kisses her deeply. He pulls her to a seating position then baths the come from her with the salt water.

"Shall we stay the night or don't you trust me?" he asks

"Oh, I trust you," she smiles

Taken

You are a sex slave. Torn from your life and just lying there on the altar. Bemused, scared, very scared. Noticing the cameras whirring and your own bare form on the screen above you.

You are left exposed. Thighs wide open and arms outstretched. Every single inch of your bareness on show in all its vulnerable glory. Even your bottom poking through a hole in the altar is caught on the screen above. Every G-spot closely filmed. Your toes, the back of your knees and your neck. Your mind drifts to those strange Japanese game shows on TV where the audience interact and decide the fate of the participant.

But your fate is already decided. You see your captor has a problem. He is badly in hoc to the local chapter of the Hell's Angels. A drug deal. Way too ambitious and his life is on the line. This is his redemption. Fresh meat. Beautiful fresh meat for the bikers. He is showing them the goods – you. If they accept the terms you are their bitch till they tire of you or until the Police find your body.

You know if they do you will be subjected to abuse beyond your wildest nightmares and your wildest, depraved fantasies. He lives for now providing they are satisfied with your performance.

Two lives at stake – his for sure, but you are yet vulnerable. The Angels have made more than a few snuff movies in their time. A lifeless performance from you will surely result in a life less. Their negotiations are now played out over a tannoy. There are no rules.

The bargain made, the doors to the hangar where you are held, are opened and the bikes roar in. The noise deafening, the theatrical revving threatening and sinister like the verbal sparring that precedes a fist fight. One by one they park and the engines are killed.

You hear a voice. The leader. The growl deep and damaged by years of heavy drinking and dust from the roads.

"You know how I want her."

The sirens, all three of them, slide from their places behind the riders and saunter to you. Looking at you more as meat than a person, they start their incredible transformation.

The first one, blonde hair and hazel eyes, is obviously the hair girl. She pulls out clippers and runs it briskly over your head. You can feel your hair fall in clumps to the floor. A short fringe is left otherwise your hair is now as short as a murderer's in Alcatraz. She pulls a cut throat and with that scratching of the blade, bares you of every remaining body hair bar your eye brows. Your arms, legs, hips, feet, pussy now smooth. She tousle's your hair free of the cuttings, sweeps the floor with her feet and leaves you to look at your new near shaven-headed self.

The second girl is the piercer. She is a Goth. Black hair, white face, black mascara and a slick of bright red lipstick. Her long talon-like nails glide over your skin, only ever a pound of pressure away from drawing blood. Her finger tips stroke each nipple until, even involuntarily, they are hard and erect. She sprays on the local anaesthetic and then threads her sharp needle through, each inserting a hoop as she goes. Then a hoop replaces your belly bar. You cry out your objection as you feel the spray applied to your pussy lips but your moan is stopped as the hair girl jerks your head back and sucks deeply on your tongue through your open mouth. Your senses shatter as her mouth sucks on you then she pulls just a little on your nipple ring, just as the needle pierces your hood. Then your feet and thighs. Implants planted under your big toes and thighs with rings screwed in. The pain subdued by the spray. The piercing siren then continues, feeding a network of chains and pulleys through each ring and stands back to admire her work. She beckons for the third siren.

The third siren is the tattooist. Inking by hand and without template. A swirl of goldfish and dragons start to cover your slightly bigger right breast, then ribs, hip and pussy. Dabbing as she goes, her speed is remarkable. The throbbing pain numbed slightly as the piercing siren strokes her talons along the un-inked skin that is left.

Within three hours your transformation is complete. You barely recognise the person you see before you. Shaven, pierced, chained, painted and just a little sore and bleeding.

Two of the girls then return to their places on the saddles. The tattooed siren drifts to the bike of their second in command. Known to the rest as Satan, he is the second in command because behind their leader he is the cruellest. Behind him sits a woman. A woman with very short hair, like one cropped and just growing back. She too is tattooed, pierced and naked. She is their previous victim. Still not entirely trusted she is now so depraved and so in lust with her life with the Angels she chooses not to leave.

The Tattoo siren takes a chain and bull whip from Satan and pulls the chain taut so the girl gags just a little. Defiance burning from her eyes, she slides from the saddle behind Satan and crawls like a leopard towards you. Purring slightly as she nears, the whip cracks across her back, reminding her of her duties. In dealing with you, her duty is to bring pleasure to her master.

Her job is to clean your wounds. Transfixed you watch as this tattooed pierced beauty folds her soft wet mouth around your big toe, sucking it lightly as if it was a little but very erect cock. Frightened more than you have ever been you may be, but the situation here is so final, your position so helpless, that your mind protects itself by allowing the pleasure to start flowing through you. Slowly, oh so slowly, she first cleans the wounds on your toes, then thighs, then your now aching nipples, before like a cat she laps at the bloodied wound of your pussy. Her tongue gliding over the ring, then the wound, then the blood that has trickled between your pussy lips and onto your clit. Her tongue flicks fast and hard. The only time it pauses is when the bull whip crashes against her and wraps itself around her waist. But your respite is temporary. The pain acts like an aphrodisiac to her and her tongue flicks ever harder and faster. Before long as you look at the screen you are no longer you. You are this twisted, painted beauty climaxing on this she-devil's mouth.

It is as you instinctively raise your knees that the chains come into play. With barely a chink of chain your nipples, clit and nearly every G-spot you have is stretched and spasms making your orgasm deeper, longer, more painful but more satisfying than you have ever had. Then she leaves and with a stroke of her head, like she is a pet, she sits once again behind Satan.

You barely have time to recapture your breath when you hear them dismounting. Not him, the leader, nor Satan, but the others. At least 8. They are all to have you before they do.

The Tattooed siren fixes a new pulley which she slowly winches. The chains tighten and slowly you are manoeuvred to where they want you to be. You are a fuck machine. Every orifice, mouth, cunt, and anus exposed for violation. Defenceless and restrained there is nothing you can do, not even call out as your head is tipped backward to receive cock, making any sound barely a gurgle.

They have one thing in common. That smell of bike oil and engine mixed with leather but otherwise they are all shapes and sizes. Your brain shuts down and your pleasure receptors go into overdrive as their hard cocks stretch, pound, fuck, thrust and lubricate every hole you have. Between the pulses of the cocks sliding from your mouth, you beg them not to come inside, but of course they do. Every one of them filling your pussy, anus or mouth.

Their previous victim lays under the altar feeding off the cum as it leaks from you like a waterfall. Then it's over. Over bar the previous victim cleaning your pussy of any last come left around your cunt. The zips are pulled tight and they head to their bikes. Tears start to flow from you, but you are not sure if it's mourning for your ruining or a celebration of the abandonment of your inhibitions.

The pulleys are again pulled and now you are sitting facing them all. Satan smiles cruelly as he looks into your eyes then sits behind you. Raising you slightly he then lowers your pussy onto his cock. You hear the excess come left by the others squelch around his cock before it is forced in a jet from your pussy. The pulleys lower him back slightly to an angle of ten o'clock.

And then it's him. You see him properly for the first time. Muscled and cruelly beautiful. His eyes make you melt. Make you ashamed. Make you wish you had saved yourself for him. Now wanting to be his, even as another man's cock is buried deep inside you.

He kicks off his boots and slides the jeans over his muscly thighs. He too smells of oil and leather, but with a hint of exotic spice. He pulls slightly at the pulley turning both you and Satan so that your cock-filled pussy is available to him. He slowly rubs the head of his cock against your cunt hole. Slowly, slowly, it stretches to allow a second cock; just the knob at first but gradually his shaft, too. He and Satan both in your pussy. You are so frightened you will tear but you don't. Your mind pictures your stretched cunt filled with those two cocks. Their shafts rubbing together, oiled by the other bikers cum, like ball bearings in a clock. The tattooed siren starts to tweak pulleys stretching your nipples and clit ever tighter. You climax almost immediately.

But it doesn't stop. Whimpering and crying, the pleasure no longer capable of being defined. Your whole body is in one shuddering constant climax as sliding against each other those cocks stretch you and fuck you. They erupt together. Filling you and smothering each other's cocks in their cum. The room echoes with the grunts and calls of all three of you.

Slowly they free themselves of you and leave you twisted, broken and wrecked on your altar. One by one the engines of the bikes roar into life and ride away. Apart from one – his.

"You coming or staying?" he says? "Well?"

The Soldier

"Well will you?" he says quietly, his soft brown eyes locked with Scarlet's dreamy far away blue pupils.

"Will I what?" Replies Scarlet shaken from her daydream.

The train had been sat for some minutes now outside Ipswich Station. Her day in the London office had been long and tiresome and after scraping the train with just seconds to spare she had secured the last available seat.

Her mind had drifted from the chores she had still to do at home, to the stations that had passed before her in such a blur she had been unable to read their place names, the dense swathes of housing finally giving way to the clusters of cows and sheep that fed on the lush green fields.

Then he had sat opposite her. Returning from duty, still uniform clad. His face a tortured reflection of the horrors he had seen. Still carrying the scars from the shrapnel wound in his cheek, the stitches merging like a river into the laughter lines around his beautiful eyes. His slightly battered helmet resting on his worn kit bag.

The other passengers had gradually disembarked at the stopping stations and now they sat alone in the carriage.

Her thoughts had drifted into a subconscious world of hedonistic delight in which she had first smiled at him enigmatically, then hitched her dress along her thighs before sinking to her knees. Slowly unbuttoning his camouflaged combats and releasing his long, hard smooth cock. Looking up at him with those sapphire blue eyes, as her tongue teases the pre come from his come hole before her soft warm wet mouth folds around his throbbing swollen purple knob. Thinking how long it must have been since he had been devoured this way.

Stroking his balls as her mouth slowly builds a rhythm along his shaft, her saliva glistening its length. Knowing he won't take long. Feeling his strong hand gently but firmly grab a handful of her hair and dictate her pace. Hearing first his gasp, then his gentle moan before that momentary pause, that final stiffening of his hips, before he comes deep into the back of her throat.

This was the side of her that no one else knew, she thought, as the previously latent slut had once again consumed her mind.

But then she had looked at the ring on her finger. He would be waiting for her. A good man if not just too settled in his ways.

"Kiss me," he asked, "Will you kiss me?"

There is a pause that seems to last forever, but then he leans forward, slowly, giving Scarlet every opportunity to murmur her objection or to put her restraining hand on his chest, but she does neither. Instead his mouth, with its day old stubble gently pricking her chin, touches hers as gently as a baby's breath.

Scarlet could still say no but she doesn't and instead allows her small mouth to open just a little and receive his tentative probing tongue.

The guilt she might otherwise feel disappearing like an early mist in the morning sun.

His hand surprisingly gentle, tenderly strokes her stockinged thigh. His hand intimately sliding under the hem of her dress and to the bare soft skin above the stocking top but going no further.

Scarlet, her tongue dancing with his, moaning gently in his mouth as the very tips of his fingers glide inside her bare thigh.

The kiss now more passionate, more driven. They both open their eyes at the same time and revel in their desire of the other and in the beauty they see.

It is only as the train jolts into life and the steward announces the imminent arrival at Ipswich, that they break their communion and smile slightly shyly at each other.

He stands and takes up his helmet and kit bag and kisses Scarlet gently on the cheek.

"Thank you, beautiful," he almost whispers in his gentle brogue.

With that he is gone.

Scarlet closes her eyes and tastes him still on her lips imagining his hands gently washing her in that hot perfumed bath.

The Threesome

You know he loves you. He tells you just as his eyes roll 20 seconds before he comes deep inside you. But he doesn't say it after. Not when he rolls away or when you place your hand on his tummy and he slides from the bed. You have counted sometimes. The real kisses. Not the times when he wants to fuck you and he slinks up behind you and gropes his hand up your top or shirt. Nor the times when you come into the lounge and he has his cock in his hand and you know he will want to guide your head onto his knob. Maybe he isn't happy either.

Maybe that is why he has been pushing for the threesome. Sex with a stranger.

He has obviously thought about it at length. He has picked her in his mind: Young, too young, blonde, tall, tanned, leggy. You have heard him wasting his effort and come masturbating in the bathroom as he pictures you and her both on your knees in front of him, mouths open like hungry birds waiting for him to feed you. You have found him trawling the net. Switching to the sports page as you come into the room. You will enjoy it he tells you. Really. Your first taste of another woman, whilst he films you both.

Actually you might. The fantasy has also been in your mind for some time. But if you decide to play. If you have a threesome. It will be on your terms.

It is at least two weeks since he last broached the subject with you. He seems to have acknowledged your indifference but you suspect he is simply hoping to slowly wear you down. That is his way. But the truth is the thought has never actually left your mind. Instead it has whirled like a carousel. Allowing that small hedonistic seed to germinate. And now not only will you let it happen, you will ensure it happens. You will arrange it. Your way. You have now trawled the sex sites he visits and seen every video he has watched. You now understand just how he wants this to unfold. You have messaged some young girls, always blonde as he wants, exchanged stories and fantasies. They have been fun. You have made sure he has seen you.

He has bitten as you knew he would. Showering as he got home, he has watched in aching anticipation from his seat at the foot of the bed as you appear in your red underwear. Making him just watch, not touch, as you use the nail scissors to roughly cut the gusset from your knickers leaving your tiny hood fully on view, lips slightly spread and clit barely protected. Placing your bare, painted toes between his spread thighs you tease the moisturiser into your smooth legs. He usually tries to look around you to catch the latest sports news when you want him, but not this time. This time you have his full attention, as you roll the hold ups till they grip your thighs.

The cab will be here in ten you whisper. He does not know how hard and fast your heart is beating in your chest. He does not know why the odd stammer creeps in. He does not know the biggest challenge is yet to come for you. He just thinks you want him and just maybe this is the night you want her, the stranger too.

The meal is good. You have said little but the few comments you have made float into his brain like perfumed foreplay. You finish your second glass. The wine has gone slightly to your head. The bar is airless. He is giving you that look, the one where mentally he is already between your legs.

"Time to go," you say.

The next moments you have planned. What happens after you have not.

You know the area behind the 'Candy Cougar Club', well since your employment in the adjoining Theatre. The Club is a well-known haunt for the lesbian and girl bi curious. He knows it, too. The 10-foot-high chicken wire separates the private VIP parking spaces from the spaces for the adjoining shops. You take him to the adjoining shop side. It is lit only by the deep blue neon signs which glow through the closed shop windows. You kiss him softly and let your fingertips gently brush over the growing bulge in his trousers.

"Your wrists," you command.

His raised eyebrows betray his nerves.

"Darling, this is the moment you've been waiting for." You whisper. "The threesome. Don't you want to play?"

A smile of acknowledgement floods across his face. You cuff his wrists to the fence then from behind release his stiff cock to the night air.

"I'll be back in five."

One of the benefits of working at the Theatre is that the bouncers at the Club and some of the regular girls are familiar faces and it costs you no more than a mild flirt with the doorman to jump the queue. Your eyes scour the dance floor. The red head with her flowing curly locks and her grinding hips initially catches your view. Then the tall blonde. Then the barely dressed brunette. Then you smile. You see me. Your temples are fit to burst as you push passed my blonde distraction, walk behind the bar where I'm serving and huskily let a hello escape your lips.

"Hi," I respond. "Can I help you?"

"Yes I think you can," you smile.

Your hand takes mine and you lead me to the door. Nothing more said between us. The cool air of the night is a welcome relief from the heat of the club.

I am not entirely comfortable. This is not my sort of game but there is something irresistibly urgent about you.

You lead me to the fence then turning your back to it our eyes meet. Our noses touch as gently as a breath before my teeth gently tug at your lower lip. Then your tongue fills my mouth. Deeper and harder. I feel your gentle moan fill my mouth as my hands slide up the front of your blouse kneading your firm full breasts. Your hand slides to my zip and releases my hard cock. Your manicured nails gently scratching my shaft and my tightening balls. You melt to your knees and like liquid chocolate, your mouth moulds around my cock. Your tongue initially massaging my filament before your lips slide their way along the length of my shaft. Then I see him for the first time. Your husband. His lips slightly parted his body restrained by the wire. His expression a mixture of jealousy and surprise but also lust and want.

"Fuck me," you whisper in my ear before biting hard on the lobe. "Don't worry I'll be back for you after tonight."

You turn and your hands reach to the fence. Your fingers entwine with his. Your nose virtually touches his. He can feel the warmth and wine on your breath.

"Is this what you wanted, baby?" you murmur.

Of course you know it's not. I am not his young blonde pussy, and yet you can feel him getting harder as his cock presses through the wire into your tummy. You feel my firm hands bend you slightly. The cool air creeps along your calves and thighs then your arse cheeks as I raise your dress. I feel you tremble slightly as I tease my fingers into your sopping wet pussy, through the hole in the gusset. I can smell your want, your lust, your need.

"Fuck me," you breathe.

You feel my swollen knob first press against then stretch your pussy. You gasp as inch by very slow inch I slide my full length inside you.

He sees your eyes close as the pleasure runs through you. He can hear as my pelvic bone bruises your arse cheeks. He can picture my cock glistening in your juices. He can smell your sweet musky juices leaking from you as your pussy muscles grip my shaft.

"Is she as lovely as you thought she'd be?" you tease. "Do you want her?" You can't help the slightly cruel smile that escapes your lips.

He looks into my eyes. We have a strange connection. We both want you, but realise you are the one who is playing us. We are your toys. He tries to look away. Your fingers tighten their grip on his.

"*WATCH*" you command. "Watch as he makes me come, watch as a real man fills my cunt with his virile, potent, baby-making come".

We have the perfect rhythm. My hands gripping your breasts tightly. So tightly they ache. My teeth biting your shoulder. Your eyes are locked with his. You see that look in his eyes. The rolling eyes just 20 seconds before he comes. You feel his warm gift land in spurts on your bare toes just as the deep intense waves of your orgasm run through you, that mix of pleasure and pain. That throbbing and deep ache inside your pussy. The heat flooding through your thighs. You feel my twitch and jerk as my cock hardens and my hot come is buried deep, deep inside you.

The pause is timeless. You and I breathless covered in a sheen of sweat through our efforts.

You turn to me, then kiss me softly and whisper

"Thursday 9 pm here. Now go."

I wander slowly and slightly dazed back to the club but look back to see you undo the cuffs. You seem strong, powerful. You slide your arm around him and whisper something soft in his ear as you lead him away. I never knew what it was you said. All I do know is that you were there Thursday and he watched, his hands cuffed to the steering wheel of his car. This time though you were all mine.

The Consequences of the End of the Affair

Every woman who has an affair with a married man knows they are playing with fire, playing with circumstances they cannot completely control. Deep down I am no different. Every night after he leaves the bed we have just fucked in, when I still smell him in the room, when my pussy has stopped throbbing from his gentle tongue, when his come can no longer be tasted on my lips, the ghouls would come.

My heart beating so fast I feel sure it will stop and bring an early death. Waves of anxiety flow through me as I lay wondering whether this might be the night she discovers our secret.

Finally, the weight of sleep overwhelms me until after a restless night my mind does what it always does. It justifies what I do, reconciles it, heals my guilt so that my want and pleasure prevail such that by the time the unwelcome beep of the alarm drags me into daytime I am ready for our next meeting, our next illicit liaison.

Of course my serenity is short lived as I enter the office. The office of Grace Solicitors LLP. Yes, I have chosen to have an affair with the husband of the senior partner of the firm in which I am a junior partner.

I say chosen. It hadn't seemed that way at first. No our first encounter had seemed like a brutal assault of my senses. The firm's Christmas cocktail party. Yes, I had noticed him. Handsome, charming, well dressed. Warming palms alongside HER, like a well-drilled escort whilst she dispensed her patronage by small words of praise or greetings of the season.

It was only when he had headed for me, when I had smelled the teasing cologne disarming my natural armour, smelled the mint on his breath that I had become drunk on his charisma.

A charisma that had let me be pushed into an empty office, had let my panties be slowly lowered to my heels, had let my skirt follow and had let him slide his long hard cock into my wet waiting pussy.

Even though I had given him my number I had not expected him to text but he had and that was six months ago now. Of course I felt guilty and at first petrified he would confess to her. Then passion and excitement had engulfed me so I cared nothing for the consequences. But now time has worn on I have begun to expect, almost want the end. The undoubtedly messy end.

I have much to lose but then I figured so did he. A wife, two children and a penthouse apartment in Chelsea. Besides as he had confided in me after a glass of wine too many she is his financial rock, his sponsor – his gallery was bust without her.

As it was, as at today we were mid row. Mid standoff. There had been rows even in our early days but now the rows had escalated. Become more prolonged more bitter. Once again he had asked me to be exclusive, his alone. Once more I had taunted him that I needed others, younger men who could give me pleasure he couldn't. It was true, well only partly.

My taunts were usually the cause of our rows. I knew they hurt him but they served a selfish purpose. Made him more detached. Detached was good. It kept him at length and gave me the excuse of not becoming any more involved than I was. Don't get me wrong I was fond of him, could easily become too fond but I was a realist. This couldn't end well.

Days would go by without a text, without an email, without a call and then he'd be there at the front door and we'd fuck. Fuck hard, fast and rough leaving us in a pool of breathless sweat.

This time though it had been two weeks. Longer than ever before. I wondered if this really was the end. Part of me felt relieved. Part of me mourned.

My usual office routine. Thursday 8 a.m. start. Log in and sip at my take away coffee whilst I reviewed the emails and calendar entries which had popped in since I had last checked my I phone before I entered the tube and my signal had been lost.

As I looked over my screen a sense of foreboding cloaked me. With the silence and stealth of a monster in a horror movie his wife, Mrs Grace was but two steps from my desk. "Coffee, Penny she commanded, say 11.30 in my office?"

Of course she knew I was free at 11.30 – she had access to my calendar. "Yes good," I said, the weight which now clogged my chest and throat, failing to influence my confident response.

It wasn't entirely unusual for Mrs Grace to want to see me I tried to assure myself. I occasionally assisted her department in their cases and of course there were appraisals and restructurings which would make our paths cross, but this felt different.

Like a prisoner knowing he would be condemned I felt an urge to rush in, to confess. Thankfully my self-survival kicked in and I am sure I appeared virtually nonchalant as I entered her room as my watch told me it was 11.30.

Any confidence I had managed to gain though drained through to my toes as she spoke.

"You are not the first, my dear," she said.

As she spoke the screen behind her flickered into life and a film slowly unwound. In a grainy black and white I watched as he fucked me. My hands gripping onto the headboard above my head, my breasts rising and falling, my mouth calling out as his cock slid in and out of me.

I sat like a small child in the Headmistress's office.

"But now it must end. He is becoming a little too distracted by you. Of course he will move on from you in the end. He always does, but that is not soon enough. I am afraid that the end will come at a cost to you, it may even bring you pain and the slut you are no little pleasure, but if you do everything I say your precious career will remain intact. Indeed, it may even lead to a promotion before your sad decision to leave us next year. Do we understand each other?"

The emotions hissed through me like lava forcing its way through the side of a volcano but I slowly swallowed it all. How dare she breach my privacy, tell me what to do, play God with my career, tell me how this will end.

I knew I needed to buy time to think this through. I needed to leave her office, to breathe fresh air again so like the compliant lamb, I demurred to the very few details she gave to me. She would email me instructions. She had my private Gmail address. Clearly she had been monitoring our exchanges of emails.

"Oh," she almost whispered as I rose "He will contact you. Tell him you are busy and offer him no encouragement. I will know if you do. "Oh and keep Saturday evening free."

The rest of the day passed in a mist containing anaesthetic. My head felt numb, my heart felt numb, my body felt numb. A supressed rage rolled around me like a marble in a pinball machine but couldn't find the will to surface. Even at home I couldn't settle spending an age trying to work out how I could so easily have been filmed. The strip of window frame with the paint removed betrayed where the camera had been taped. I reached for the bottle of brandy and remember nothing after the third tumbler.

I woke feeling much better than I had any right to. I was late for work but didn't care. During the night my mind had done what it did best. It reconciled all that had gone on the day before and had settled my thoughts into a positive spin. We were finished me and him. That was clear, but then I knew it was going to end soon anyway. He would be okay. They had clearly survived his other indiscretions. I actually wanted it to end. Yes, she had found out, but hey I was still alive. She hadn't sacked me or marched me from the building. In fact, and I believed her, If I did what she said I would come out of this okay. Like she said I would no doubt be moved on but if I played this right she would find me a suitable practise. This game worked both ways. She wouldn't want the world knowing she was such a frigid bitch her husband needed to fuck me.

My weary eyes reached for my mobile and scanned the texts and emails. Amongst the texts was one from him, "I miss you, we can sort this, let me see you Sunday?"

My tummy clenched, part of me wished I could take him into my confidence and tell him what had happened, but I had my instructions ringing in my ears. Besides it was time for this to end and if I had to play some bizarre game to do it then so be it.

I replied simply, "Soon maybe but not this weekend. I am away x."

I turned to my emails intending to email my secretary that I was sick, and wouldn't be in when HER email popped into my inbox.

"P Do not come into the office today. I have made an appointment for you with my stylists at Benedicts at four. They have their instructions. Follow them. Remember keep Saturday evening free from seven. Has he been in touch? G."

My only focus was on her question. Telling her the truth would be a betrayal of the intimacy we had enjoyed. But his relationship, this sexual liaison however much fun it had been had to end. My career had to survive whatever the price. I swallowed and closed my eyes so that I could not see as I copied his text and my response to her.

"P, well done. I see we understand each other," G.

At 4 p.m. I find myself in Benedict's, the exclusive hairdressing, beauty salon and spa used only by the wealthy and famous, however temporary. I sit for a short while in their reception whilst the odd vaguely familiar face from the gossip magazines are greeted by incredibly beautiful assistants and led into what I imagine are the temples of pleasure beyond.

I am soon greeted by a woman who makes my pussy ache. Did I not mention my bi tendencies? French, smouldering, olive skinned and soft Gallic accent that sounds like every word is a kiss. I barely hear her greetings, her acknowledgement that I am a special guest of Mrs Grace that my hair will be done by Michael, that she will then be responsible for the beauty treatments that have been requested. I don't recall declining her offer of champagne or accepting her offer of coffee. In my head her thighs are parted and my tongue laps at her with little kitten licks.

Before my fantasy can go any further I am greeted by Michael an utterly beautiful, charming, camp, bouffant of creativity. The motive for my visit, what may be sinister reasons for this makeover are lost on me. I am here to be moulded, to be shaped. I am happy to be both.

Before long I see clips of my long dark hair fall to the salon floor. It is only then I realise there is not a single mirror. The hair that has taken me years to grow is lying in a heap on the floor. I have no idea how I will look. A colour is applied. I have no idea what colour. Finally, Michael delivers his judgment. It is perfect. It is just what Mrs Grace wanted.

"Can I see," I ask hopefully

"You know Mrs Grace doesn't want you to see yet, naughty," is Michael's response.

I am led through to my fantasy. She obviously realises I took little notice during our first conversation and re-introduces herself as Simone. Her nimble fingers and pots and potions are soon sculpting, stripping and smoothing my face and body. Again not a mirror in sight.

"I'm sorry, but as you know you cannot see what happens next," she virtually breathes into my mouth as she gently places the blindfold over my eyes.

I feel a slight shame as I feel her slide my panties from me. Shame partly because I haven't shaved in the two weeks since I haven't been speaking with him, and partly because my glistening pussy must betray the want I have for her. I gasp slightly as the wax is pulled from reluctant skin.

I try to picture what she is doing. Not all of the hair has gone. She shapes what is left with tiny clippers. I feel her paint liquid on the remaining hair then slowly rinse me clean. Her fingers tousling through the short hair as the shower rinsing me sends a tingle through my spine and a deep need through my bare exposed pussy.

"Shh… I have some cream relax," her fingers gently stroke the newly bare skin with the cream. I come silently as she gently kneads the same cream into my swollen pink pussy lips. Does she know? Is that why she gently holds my fingers till my breathing subsides?

Michael breaks the spell as he enters the studio in a wave of happiness and compliments.

"Beautiful, beautiful, beautiful," he virtually applauds. "Now it's time for you to see."

I am led to a small room where every wall, the floor, and the ceiling are mirrored. It's not me. The woman who stares back at me is not me. Gone is the long straight black hair replaced by wavy shoulder length red/copper hair with matching eyebrows. My lips are plumped and full. My black pubic hair now shaped into a red/copper heart. My toenails and fingernails now painted a winter soft brown.

"Wow," is all I can truly say. I remain in the same state of bemused excitement until I find myself soaking in my bath at home sipping a glass of wine laughing out loud like a demented hyena.

My next mail arrives late evening.

"P I hear you enjoyed Simone – oh and Michael. Being a slut will hold you in good stead for what lies ahead. A parcel will arrive at yours at 11.00 a.m. You will dress in the clothes I provide. I have your sizes. Be at the Royal Hotel bar at 7 p.m. Wait till you are contacted – G."

The same supressed anger rolls like an undercurrent through me. How dare the bitch judge me? "Frigid cow," I hiss at the phone screen.

As I lay wearily in my bed my subconscious finally starts to work. Is this about revenge? Maybe? Clearly whatever she has planned is designed to finish he and I but why the makeover? Why do I need to be a slut – the last question is the last thought that rolls through my mind, as I reach between my legs and imagine Simone sucking gently on my hard nipples whilst she rubs soft lubricating cream on my aching clit.

I wake to the sound of my front door bell. I quickly check the alarm clock.

Shit I've slept in. Its eleven o'clock.

I pull on my dressing gown, ruffle my fringe and open the door. It's Bob, one of the couriers from the office.

"Morning Miss, a delivery from Graces LLP for you."

"Very formal this morning, Bob," I retort in response to what I assume is his mock formality.

"I'm sorry, Miss, do I know you?"

I shrug awkwardly sign for the parcel and close the door quickly. I then catch my reflection in the mirror.

"Oh my God," I exclaim. "No wonder Bob doesn't recognise me. I don't recognise me. I'm that stunning fucking gorgeous, red head.

I need calm. I do not bath till five then using the tips given by Michael recreate the sway of my hair. It is not till six that I open the parcel. It contains only five items. A long elegant green silk dress, gold strappy heels, ivory hold ups, matching high cut silk ivory knickers and several pairs of green contact lenses – in my prescription.

I have to say I am starting to admire Mrs Grace. She plays dirty, really dirty, but she does her research. I dress slowly, almost like it's a date with a new boyfriend. I simply don't recognise the girl I am now. A natural elegant smouldering siren of a red head. I am not me. I am Red. I smile at myself in the mirror. "Hello Red."

My nerves nearly consume me as at ten minutes to seven my taxi drops me a short way before the Hotel. I pace up and down. I have a need to run. A need to pee. A need to cry. But here I am dutifully on time at the south end of the bar at the Royal Hotel.

"Ah, madam," says the bar tender in an accent that sounds like all of those used in the Mediterranean rolled into one.

"I have your order. Please that is your table. I will bring your drink."

The flute of champagne is duly delivered only moments after I sit. A second one appears just as soon as the first is finished. It is now 7.15.

"Hello, Penny," I know the voice before I turn. It is Gerald Bartholomew. The Vice President – Mrs Grace's Rottweiler – her enforcer.

"Mr Bartholomew," I say, my voice not disguising my surprise.

"Tonight, dear, it is Gerald. May I join you?"

I think his request is little more than manners on his part as he is already looking to slide the chair back to ease his passage next to me.

"We need to leave shortly, my dear. I have been sent to make sure you are ready and can I say you are nearly perfect."

"Only nearly?" I nervously joke.

"You have forgotten the lenses. Please go put them in and then we can leave."

I hate that I have forgotten them. I had planned to put them in on my arrival, but my nerves have over taken me.

I retire to the ladies' room and put in the twinkling green lenses. If I had thought the transformation was complete before, it was now. I give myself a small enigmatic smile of approval. My view is confirmed as soon as Bartholomew sees me.

"Now you are perfect, my dear."

Bartholomew stands and takes me by the hand. He steers me from the bar to the foyer with a gentle pressure from his finger on my elbow alone. Mrs Grace's personal driver awaits us outside and quickly opens doors for us both.

"You know where we are going," Bartholomew says firmly.

There is something about Bartholomew that arouses lust and displeasure in me in equal measure. Silver haired, lithe, commanding, a fixer, a controller, a quite beautiful authority fantasy. Yet he scares me. The way he looks at me, not just now, but before all this started, leaves me uneasy. I don't know where his boundary line lies. Whether I am simply expendable fodder despite the apparent concern and mentoring. I think that I would risk simply being fodder to pleasure him is the last thought I have before the car stops.

"The office?" I question,

"As quick and as insightful as ever I see," he dryly murmurs before we walk into the reception. The desk is empty. It would seem the 24-hour concierge has been given the evening off.

I am guided to the receptionists' rest room and he turns me gently to face him.

"You have been a silly girl, Penny, but Mrs Grace is good to her word. See this through fully with a willing body and mind and what she promised you, you will get. If you don't she will finish all you hold dear, her anger and ability to punish is without limit."

"Will I get hurt? – whatever it is," I ask betraying my one real fear,

"I suspect not," he says smiling almost wickedly "to be honest if you are half the person I suspect you to be, you will probably enjoy it. Now two final additions and they will be ready for you."

"They."

"Yes they I have a small number of friends and associates with me, from my Club."

My mind races, failing to process quite what could be expected of me, failing to process an exit route

"Please calm yourself," he continues "let me finish your preparation then we should hasten to our guests."

From behind him Bartholomew presents a gold diamanté opera mask which he fixes with Velcro.

"That will help protect your anonymity, Penny," he assures.

"Does it need protecting?"

"Yes of course, your punishment is harsh but fair. It is not intended to ruin your career."

He reaches behind him again and pulls out a handwritten sign on string that he places over my neck. It says simply

"I cannot speak. Use me as you will."

"Can you really not tell me what awaits me?" I hear myself plead.

He tenderly takes my head in his hands, "No I cannot but I will give you one small clue. Remember we have seen all of the emails that have passed between you both. It would seem that the thought of this is something you have a strong desire to experience. Oh I nearly forgot – he adds – If we have misjudged you use the word "Augustus.""

I obviously look confused as he feels the need to explain.

"Inappropriately it is my father's name, but today it is your safe word. It is the only word you can utter. If you do the night will immediately come to an end, but be warned use it only if you want this to end as you will have failed. Now I will leave you. Wait five minutes and enter the main boardroom. There will be a desk. Stand with your back to it and wait."

Bartholomew's clear blue eyes peer into mine searching my soul for my acknowledgement of his terms and for my consent of what is to come.

I shudder just slightly under his gaze feeling sure that at that single moment I want him. I want Gerald Bartholomew's cock deep inside me. I finally nod to confirm my consent.

I count to what I believe to be five minutes. In real time it might not have been more than two or three. My mind is now a blur, my heart is racing, my mouth is dry.

This is it. I go through the door or run. Run and Mrs Grace will effectively end my career. I have no doubt she has the power and influence to do so. Run and I may miss out on something I crave. Bartholomew's words still rang in my ears. Run and avoid closure? Whatever this is, it brings the affair and the ensuing punishment to an end.

I know in my heart I have no desire to run. Of the three reasons my inner want and curiosity is in control. I want to know why Bartholomew and Grace think I will enjoy this. I want to know why I have been transformed. I enter the long deep rectangular room. It is dark bar some gentle diffused lighting on the floor to my left.

The leather musky smell of the books fills the air but it is the only thing that is familiar. In place of the long boardroom table is a simple single desk or table covered in a gold silk cloth making it look like an altar. As instructed I stand with my back to it. I hear the door to my right open and hear and smell rather than see the people enter. I hear chairs pulled, and then they sit all four of them. The only thing I can see are four pairs of feet dressed in polished brogues and turned up bottoms of expensive tailored suits.

I feel faint and realise I have held my breath since I entered the room. Silence!

I can feel the eyes of these four men taking me in. If vision was water, I would be drenched from head to toe.

"Perfect," I hear one murmur.

And I am. I have parked my feisty feminist independent woman of the world. Tonight, I am not me I am Red. A receptor of pleasure and I will be whatever these men want, as long as they satisfy my needs, too. The need that has grown deep in me, as this experience has unfolded.

The door opens again and someone else enters. They do not sit, but I feel them approach me slowly. She is close before I recognise her. It is Simone, the beautician from Benedict's.

This I didn't expect. She smiles at me reassuringly then whispers gently in my ear, "I know that you came when I stroked you. Tonight I get to play with you how I really want to."

She lifts the sign from over my head and lays it on the floor.

She is very slightly shorter than me and my eyes hold hers as they get closer and closer. I feel her soft honey breath blow gently on my mouth till my lips open, craving the touch of hers.

Her lips are firm with just a hint of give. They gently pincer my lower lip and tease it away from me. I am enthralled, in awe. I want this woman to use me in any way she wants.

Her lips then pincer my top lip before they press firmly against mine. My mouth opens to receive her and her long thin pink tongue searches the wetness of my mouth. My tongue tries to meet hers, to dance and tangle with hers but she is in control. Every time her tongue slides in my mouth it feels like it is penetrating my tight but soaking pussy. I let out an involuntary groan as my pussy spasms and clenches, releasing yet more come down the bare tops of my thighs.

She breaks from me, leaving me panting deep breaths and gives my lips a small sharp peck. I feel her fingers undermine the protection of my dress strap, the thin thread of silk teasing my shoulder and upper arm as she slides it down, until it pulls with it, the right side of my dress leaving my breast bare.

I feel her wet mouth suck on my neck under my chin. Then a mixture of small but beautifully painful sucks and bites along my cleavage and the mounds of my full firm breast. The closer her mouth gets to my nipple the more my pussy spasms. I reach for myself I cannot help it. Through the fine silk my nails stroke the outside of my pussy lips. Simone's tongue teases the tip of my nipple before her soft wet mouth engulfs it all, holding the shaft of the nipple firm whilst her tongue massages the tip.

I push my fingers through the protection of my outer lips and let the cool silk act like a luxuriant lube as my fingers gently massage my clit. My waves quickly build but my rhythm is stopped as I feel the other strap slipped over my shoulder and the dress slide slowly to the floor.

I watch as the men's shoes shuffle. I feel sure I hear a zip lowered. I know that all of them want me. They are watching every moment, every inch of me.

Using only a gentle but firm kiss and the weight from her own breasts Simone backs me onto the altar and I recline under the sheer ecstasy of her mouth on mine. I hear my involuntary protests then moans of pleasure as her soft kisses and gentle licks work their way along my breasts tummy and hips before I sense her kneeling between my legs as if readying herself to pray. I feel my thighs spread and my knickers very slowly pulled down over my hips, then along the full length of my legs, and over my heels snagging slightly as they do. My glistening bare pussy lips now on full display to the mysterious voyeurs.

Her tongue cleans the come coating my thighs, her fingers lowering the tops of my hold ups to ensure none is missed. My body jolts as if shaken as she rips at the thighs of each hold up as they obscure the target of her desires. I cannot see her, but I close my eyes and picture the mouth of this beautiful woman drifting between the tatters of the torn silk.

Then I feel her gentle breath blowing on my reddened swollen pussy lips. Then a little harder. Her slim fingers spreading my lips like they are a ripened fig, opening my fruit to her and the audience. She opens my cunt and lets her finger roll around the outside before I feel first her manicured nail then finger penetrate me. I hear her suck her finger coated in my come.

"You really are delicious," she murmurs.

Her finger re-enters me and curls in search of my G spot. I feel my back arch and pussy grind on her almost of their own accord to make the perfect angle. I start to buck as the heavy deep aching waves build within me as she massages my magical spot. She senses my orgasm is near, my breath fast and short, thighs gently trembling

"Not yet, my beautiful," she whispers "I want you to come under my mouth.

Her withdrawn come-coated finger rolls around my hot red throbbing clit. I swallow my breath as I feel her wet mouth fold around it. Her saliva joining my own sex juices as a thin film of lubrication. Her tongue never losing contact, alternating between a firm pressured rolling massage and gentle sharp flicks like a kitten drinking milk.

My mind takes me into a lustful depraved utopia, and it is then just as my orgasm is about to explode and burn its deep heat through my pussy and thighs that I know what I want.

I want four cocks, hard long thick cocks fucking every hole that I have.

My mind trips and my animalistic groan echoes around the room and back to me as my body seizes and jerks and the orgasm shudders through me. I have no concept of time or place as the waves slowly subside with Simone drinking the come that freely flows from me.

"That was quite astonishing, my dear, you really are quite stunning."

I have not registered Simone's departure or Bartholomew's arrival. My eyes flicker to clear the blur and I see his blue eyes piercing the veneer of armour I have left by way of defences.

"Now it is time for you to entertain your guests."

The tone is matter of fact but it is clearly a command rather than an invitation.

My eyes are level with his crotch and I instinctively reach to stroke him through his suit trousers. Even with the slightly baggy cut that he wears I feel a hard but short bulge. My hands fold as far around it as they can go and pressing my palm firmly against the shaft slowly wank him from base to tip.

I see the pleasure I bring in the flicker in his eyes, the very slight change in this cool dapper man's breath, the substantial change in the hardness of his cock.

As if reading my mind, he undoes his waist button and lowers his zip. I had till now wanted this man based upon his cool detached authority softened by his occasional moments of compassion, but now I wanted the thickest cock I have ever seen, which has just sprung from its secure hiding place. He smiles at my surprise.

My hands truly cannot fold entirely around its girth. He edges forward and his big swollen pink knob with its tiny tear of pre cum leaking from its slit is resting against my lips.

Even taking in this beautiful tip stretches my mouth and I need to adjust my angle and the moisture in my mouth before inch by slow inch the hardness fills the soft wetness of my mouth. The length is not the difficulty for me, but the width stretches my cheeks and I fear I may resemble a horny puffer fish.

Slowly we build a rhythm. He doesn't try to fuck my mouth but lets me slowly slide to the base of the shaft letting my tongue tease his sensitive filament on the return journey.

I feel hands on me but I cannot turn to see. Fingers gently stroking across my tensed tummy before gently kneading my left breast, more fingers on my right breast firmly pinching my nipple causing a hot rush through to my pussy. Now yet more fingers holding my pussy lips wide apart, I am defenceless, unable to control the sensations being inflicted on me.

Warm lube is poured over my clit and slowly, softly, the fingers massage me. My pleasure is entirely in the gift of these men. In my mind I see lots of hands, 10 or 20 all pulling at me, caressing me, teasing me.

My hands are now guided by the men playing with my breasts onto their bare semi hard cocks. My hands slowly pump them fully in to life whilst my mouth works Bartholomew's cock, my saliva now the thinnest barrier between his skin and mine.

An unseen signal and Bartholomew withdraws his cock form me, stroking my hair and cheek and my lips as silent but fulsome praise.

He is slowly replaced by three longer thinner cocks; the ones I have made hard. I cannot see much beyond them but one by one they are offered to my mouth and one by one I take them.

My spittle glistening off every one as my head is turned first one way then another to pleasure them.

My legs are opened wider. It must be Bartholomew. His huge knob presses against my oiled cunt. Despite the lube I feel stretched like never before as slowly, almost in slow motion, he inserts just the knob. I feel my groan vibrating against the cock in my mouth.

Bartholomew's fingers gently massage my aching clit as very slowly he edges the rest of his thick shaft into me. It is painful but I like it. A deep throbbing pain that grows until his full shaft is inside me. I need to breathe, to pant until my pussy settles. I keep the three cocks at the tip of my tongue then take the first back in as slowly Bartholomew withdraws then re-enters, every time filling me like no one ever has.

I am so stretched I feel my clit dragged down till it is virtually rubbing against his shaft. Every time he re-enters me the base of his shaft slaps against it sending waves of aching pleasure through me. I am in a depraved ecstasy. Hands touching me feeling me, groping me. My mouth stuffed with hard cock as soon as another leaves it.

The waves of orgasm are deeper than anything I have experienced. I feel like my body is no longer my own. My orgasm will not stop, it goes on and on. The deep aches of heat and pleasure continuing to run through my tummy, my thighs, my cunt.

A hand pulls my hair back and roughly guides it so I am now looking at the ceiling and that's when I see him. HIM! He is one of the four. Our eyes briefly lock. I look for a sign, a flash of recognition but there is none. He simply pumps his cock towards his impending orgasm.

I simply cannot absorb his involvement – not now. I feel Bartholomew driving harder and as deep as he can into my pussy. I can smell the men around me ferociously pumping their cocks above my face. I partially close my eyes. I don't want to see their faces. I just want to see their cocks spurting their jets of come all over me. I hear myself let out a long deep primitive groan that is quickly echoed by Bartholomew as I feel his cock pulse before releasing his hot come deep inside me.

A grunt from a man above me and I feel his come hit my lower lip and neck, then more come sprays like warm treacle across my mouth and my breasts. Jet after jet of warm sticky treacle as each of them come over me.

I lay there catching my breath, my mind trying to process all of the pleasures to which I have been subjected, his involvement nagging through the throbbing pleasure like a maggot in an apple.

I sense the men drifting away and soon I am alone with heat in my body and small fountains of cold come dripping from it.

"Come, my dear, put this on," I focus on Mrs Grace holding a dressing gown stretched wide for me to slide into. I slowly raise myself and allow her to wrap the robe around me and dab my face with a damp towel.

"I have something to show you."

She leads me by the hand into her private office. She sits in her smart two-piece suit and lowers me like a child newly woken from sleep onto her lap where she holds me tenderly, her fingers comforting my lower thighs.

He enters and pours himself a whisky from her private cabinet and then turns surprised to see us both. He smiles at her nervously but still has not a flicker of recognition for me. "What are you doing here?" I hear the break in his voice.

"Working a little late, dear," she says calmly. He turns to leave but has barely moved before she says "Don't go yet I want you to see something." With a click of the remote control, the screen behind her desk flickers into life and I am there being fucked, filled, squeezed and groped by them all. The sight is more horny than I had ever thought possible.

I feel no shame then only a deep desire for it all to happen again but without HIM.

But then the film continues. My entire transformation has been filmed. We all watch as Bartholomew places the mask and sign on me, how he meets me at the hotel, through to my long straight black hair falling at Michael's feel before it is transformed into its copper/red and finally in the office of Mrs Grace when she first exposes me as his lover.

I watch him as he watches the film. The tumbler never reaches his lips. He looks at me and then at her. I watch as the end of their marriage unfolds whilst the film plays in silence.

"You lost me some time ago, Robert, now you have lost her, too."

My lawyers will be in touch with you. I have booked you into the Crowne Plaza at Blackfriars. You will find the things you need there."

He is too traumatised to speak to argue or plead. He places the tumbler on the table and leaves.

I do now feel guilt, the weight of this marital demise on my shoulders and conscience. She seems to read my mind.

"You have been a very foolish girl, Penny, but as I said before you are not the first and you would not have been the last. Your punishment has been delivered. You did as I asked and you have taken the punishment well. I have decided to wipe the slate clean between us. You will be useful to us here at Grace LLP."

I look up at her soft brown eyes and feel not a moment of hesitation in opening my mouth as her lips touch mine…

And that is where my affair with the wife of my former lover and the senior partner of the Law firm where I am a junior partner begins.

The Pawnbroker

"A Pawnbroker is an individual or business that make loans to people with items of personal property used as collateral or security. If an item is pawned the customer must repay the loan with interest by the date agreed. If he does the item is returned to him. If he does not the item is sold by the Pawnbroker to recover his money."

Harry Squires is the last in a long line of Pawnbrokers. The business originally started by his great grandfather Harold, has lent money to those in ready need of cash in the East End for over 70 years.

The three golden balls hanging from their shop had been a magnet for those without access to conventional sources of lending such as Banks and Building Societies.

But in more recent times business had become tough. The competition from cash conversion companies and the ready availability of credit elsewhere had squeezed their margins ever tighter and left them as a funder of last resort.

Harry had kept his opinions on how the business should be run to himself, ever respectful of his elderly father's traditional views. But within months of his father's death he had sold the lease of the shop to a leading supermarket chain and taken on a small plush studio in Mayfair.

You see Harry was still a pawnbroker. He still lent money, but unlike his father and his family before him, Harry did not take items of property as collateral. Harry took people as security

If you were to repay his loan, then like property, the person you had tendered as security was released from their obligation. But if you did not repay the loan they became Harry's.

The customer then had fourteen days more to repay but now at an expensive rate of interest. In those fourteen days Harry would start to train his new possession.

If the loan with the penalty interest was not repaid within these fourteen days, then Harry would sell them. Sell them to his network of private and wealthy buyers to use as they will.

That person would always be returned in the end, if they wanted to be.

It was these very terms that Harry had made clear to Mr and Mrs Kiss as they had sat before him just two weeks before.

His face had tried not to betray his excitement as yet another body and soul would become his to facilitate its use, to exploit and torture.

He took in her nervous features as his cigar smoke curled like claws towards her. Difficult to age, maybe forty maybe forty-five. Beautifully presented with her feline features and mid length blonde hair especially done for the day. She needn't have bothered as she would see. Slim, but with wide hips and full breasts. Long legs and small tight ankles. He could almost feel himself purring inside.

"But I never thought you would really hold me to those terms," the nondescript Mr Kiss protested.

Harry had heard this protest many times before. He reached inside his locked filing cabinet and pulled out their file. Amongst the papers inside is a brown envelope. He opens it and starts to lay out the photos like a deck of cards onto the desk. The photos of Scarlet, Mrs Kiss. The ones she had been required to have taken when the loan was first made.

Harry takes a long drag on his cigar, and rocks back in his chair remembering the photo shoot. Her slow corruption had been one of his favourites. He could not help but let his fingers fall to the bulge growing between his legs.

"You are free to leave if you wish, but you will still owe me the money. Oh and I'm sure your employers would be very interested in these, Mrs Kiss."

Scarlet's eyes flash towards her husband's defeated features.

"You can put those away, Mr Squires. I am very well aware of what I have signed up to," says Scarlet calmly.

"But, dear..."

"Norman, I would suggest you concentrate on raising the money we are required to pay Mr Squires."

And so her training had begun...

Pandora checked him through the screen on her desk connected to the CCTV.

Cute, sharply dressed in expensive suit, shirt and tie.

"I am here to see Mr Squires. My appointment is at 11."

His soft deep brogue sends a naughty shiver through her spine. A shiver that turns into a steady tremble as his tall, slim, but toned frame, pushes through the buzzing door and with crisp steady footsteps he makes his way to her desk.

"Can I offer you a drink, Mr Black?" Pandora offers in a less than assertive tone.

"No I'm fine, but thank you."

"Please take a seat, I'll tell Mr Squires you are here."

Pandora rises, escorts Black to the sleek black leather sofa then disappears through a door immediately behind her desk.

Black looks and rightly suspects that at least one panel of the blackened partition is two-way glass and that he is being watched.

Pandora is gone for two minutes, maybe more, before she reappears.

"Mr Squires will see you now," she breathes.

She waits for Black to join her then leads him into the office beyond.

The office that is a stark contrast to its reception. Bar the glass one adjoining the reception, the walls are wood panelled, broken sporadically by bookcases housing ancient books. The room is furnished with slightly worn and tattered but exquisite tan leather chairs and sofas and is lit only by two small desk lamps such that the shadows hide its corners.

"Mr Black, it is good to see you again."

"Mr Squires."

As the two men shake hands, Black takes in the features of his host. Maybe in his early sixties, grey, thinning hair sleeked back. Pinched face, thin frame. An air of the Headmaster, the disciplinarian.

"Please take a seat, let me pour us some tea and then you can tell me how I can help you."

The two men sit, and Squires reaches to the cups and teapot, he pours a cup for them both.

"Milk?"

"No I take mine black, thank you."

Squires clicks his fingers and from the shadows strides a woman. A red head, petite with sparkling green eyes. She unbuttons her blouse till her breasts are bared then kneels before Squire's cup.

His manicured hand slowly manipulates her slightly reddened mound then her pink swollen nipple. Squires murmurs a deep groan of pleasure as the milk jets from her nipple into his cup.

"Thank you, Gretel."

As if knowing her duties have been performed to her owners' satisfaction, Gretel re-buttons her blouse and retires to the shadows.

Black is well travelled and has seen much. The sight arouses him but does not distract him.

"So who do you have that is new to me?" asks Black.

With a swipe of his hand over the arm of his chair another corner of the room is lit. A woman, tall and slim, in gimp outfit stands still staring ahead, a lit bulb cupped in her hands.

"As you know 'Compliance is everything', Mr Black. Sylvia there is my star pupil. Only when they reach this standard do they go to sale, she is available to you."

Black reaches for his tea and that is when he sees Scarlet for the first time. She is the table. She is on all fours. Naked bar the clear glass surface strapped to her back. Her head is bowed.

"Ah, Scarlet," Squires admonishes. "Scarlet is sadly one of my slower learners, she regrettably needs further work."

Squires reaches into the gap between the cushion and chair frame and pulls out a metal shock wand. Black has seen and felt these. The wand that dispenses electric shocks like a human cow prod. He almost winces as Squires brushes it lightly along the top of Scarlet's bare thighs and exposed pussy lips. The shock makes her rattle the cups, tea pot and milk jug and jolt the hot well of wax from the candle sitting on the edge of the table on to her lower thighs, calves and soles of her feet.

She makes not a sound, not a whimper. She just tilts her head, her beautiful sapphire blue eyes staring into Black's soft brown eyes. Her teeth bite deep into her soft pink lower lip.

"How much do you want for her?" Black asks.

"Who?"

Black nods nonchalantly in Scarlet's direction.

"I'm afraid, Mr Black, she is not for sale. She is not yet ready."

"As you know I like my horses unbroken."

"My other customers pay very much more for the broken compliant type I'm afraid."

"How much?"

"She is not ready."

"One day. I want her for one day. There will be two of us."

"You are very determined."

"£5,000. No rules, no boundaries."

"You cannot kill her or break her."

"I said no rules, no boundaries."

"£10,000 and you can do with her what you will."

The price is higher than he would normally want to pay but he cannot resist.

"I'll pay it. I want her the day after tomorrow." Black notices the wedding ring still adorning Scarlet's finger. "Oh and her husband watches."

"2 p.m.? You know the payment terms. I will require the money into my account by 10 a.m. tomorrow."

"It will be there."

"Then we have an agreement, Mr Black."

Black rises, shakes Squires hand and leaves.

The next morning Squires confirms to Scarlet that the payment has been made. He tells her coldly and with a hint of menace not to let him down. He has a reputation to maintain and Mr Black is a valued client. He smiles cruelly before telling her how he looks forward to watching the film of her violation.

The day arrives. The other girls shave her of all bodily hair then bathe her. Their knowing smiles as their fingers slip between her hood and feel the soaking wet cunt beyond.

Her hair is waxed slick back, her lips painted a bright whore red. The lipstick is applied to her pink nipples then the word written across her hips – "MEAT."

She is cuffed to a wooden crucifix and wrapped in a black bin bag type material.

With the crucifix heavy on her shoulders she is led into the studio. Once there they make her wait. Her heart beats fast, the fear now running through every nerve ending. The anticipation both arousing and disturbing.

The blade of the Stanley knife held by Squires cuts through the plastic just inches from her face and body.

Like cargo she is unwrapped and presented to the room.

Her eyes take a little while to adjust to the studio. The first thing she notices are the clusters of candles alight on the silver candelabras. The flames creating a church like mood, the heat flaming her bareness. The second thing she sees is her husband, his trousers and pants around his ankles, bound to an old fashioned armchair.

His eyes almost pitiful. He has the perfect view of the black silk clad bench in the middle of the room.

The two of them enter from a door to the side. Black, the one she has seen before, sits on the bench. The second man, approaches her. He kisses her softly, then pulls a wand from his belt. He clicks a button on its shaft and an attachment of soft brushes flicks from its tip. With a click of another button they start to rotate in irregular movements. The brushes tease her neck, tummy and hips. He watches as her eyes flash as the tingles run through her. Her breathing becomes slower and heavier and then, knowing he has her full attention he stops. Smiling to himself, he turns to his holdall and pulls out two large metal spiders, much like a scalp massager. In the middle of each is a small clamp. Taking each breast in turn, he puts the small clamps over the nipple and tightens it until it is tight enough to hold the entire spider contraption in place. Tightens it until Scarlet gasps as the deep tortuous throb makes her entire breast and tummy ache.

He pulls a control switch with wires from the bag and plugs a wire into each spider.

"Ready," he says before smiling at Black.

Black heads to the holdall and pulls out his own bundle of wires and toys.

He walks to Scarlet and kisses her softly initially, but then harder and deeper until her defenceless frame is left breathless. He sinks to the floor and places tiny silk like hoods over each of her big toes. He then attaches small pads to the back of her knees and lastly he eases a plug lubricated only by his own saliva, into her anus.

Each accessory is then wired to his control box. Black sits on the bench. His eyes lock with Scarlet's as he slowly turns the control knobs on each. The effect is immediate. Her body jerks upright as the sensors tease her G spots. Her toes tingle as the hoods pleasure them like tiny cat tongues and the spiders massage and knead her breasts. The clamps tighten and stretch like hungry mouths feeding. The butt plug ejects warm oils like come deep into her anus.

The second man reactivates his wand and holds it gently against Scarlet's hood.

"Has she ever begged for you?" the second man asks Mr Kiss.

Mr Kiss's head sinks into his chest. The second man can see Scarlet's resistance has gone; she may even come without the wand breaking through the hood.

"Please," Scarlet moans,

"Beg."

"Please."

"Beg."

"Please, I beg you."

The man eases the brushes gently through her hood such that it now rests on the hard and aching clit beyond. Within seconds the climax shudders its hot and aching way through Scarlet's pussy, thighs and tummy. Her body twitches and convulses whilst her brain tries to make sense of the complete pleasure to which her senses have been subject.

Still breathless and limp she is released from the toys and wires and laid on her back across the bench where her eyes lock with her husband's.

Her eyes close only seconds later as Black's wet warm mouth closes around her clit and his tongue slowly massages her. As her eyes open she looks to the second man. He pulls a pistol from his bag and slides out the chamber. The waves of pleasure slowly engulf her as he ejects the bullets until the chamber is empty. He then places only one bullet back in the chamber and spins it. Her hips buck as the surreal scene plays havoc with the sensibilities in her mind and Black's tongue plays havoc with her clit. She grinds her cunt deep into his face as the second man looks at her kindly, puts the barrel to her temples and pulls the trigger – "Click."

That's one.

The rush pushes her to orgasm and as her focus blurs she sees her husband, still looking pitiful, but with his cock now hard and throbbing.

The second man gently pulls Scarlet to her feet whilst Black lays on his back on the bench sliding a cushion under his buttocks. Scarlet straddles him her soaking wet hole embracing Black's helmet. Slowly she lowers herself onto his long length, her husband helpless to stop just a dribble of white come escaping his come hole.

He sees the pleasure on his wife's face as this stranger fucks her. Her very life out of his control. She slides her pussy up and down his shaft seeing in her eyes the pleasure she brings to him. She smiles then steadies herself with her hands around his throat.

Squeezing softly at first then a little harder until she feels the first moment he gags for air. He slides a single stocking from his side, ties a knot in the middle then ties it around her neck so the knot is pressed against her oesophagus. He pulls it tighter until she too pauses for breath. Then she starts to ride him.

She feels the second man teasing her anus with lube. A single finger gently slides in and then slowly out of her and then again, but this time she realises it is too hard, too cold to be a finger. It is the barrel of the pistol.

Each time she sinks to the base of Black's cock, she also sinks lower onto the barrel.

"Click."

That's two. She pauses briefly as she realises the chamber is empty again then rides him faster and harder. The stocking tightening a little more around her pale slim neck.

"Click."

Three. Scarlet looks at her husband, the come now rolling along his shaft like melted ice cream.

Her tiny hands now fix tighter around Black's throat. Her buttocks slamming harder into his pelvis, the handle of the gun pressed tightly into Black's balls.

"Click."

That's four.

Their vision becoming blurred through the force they are slowly applying on each other's throat. The pleasure becoming more intense, more distinct.

"Click."

That's five. Just one more to go. The death bullet from the barrel still deep inside her anus.

Scarlet squeezes tighter. Black squeezes tighter. Her pussy muscles tighten around his shaft. She can feel the waves building inside her. Waiting for that moment. The moment when the bullet erupts inside her.

"Click."

That's six. The chamber is empty but the sheer rush and adrenalin makes her come deeper and harder than she ever has before. Black calls out in a loud animalistic roar as with one last effort his pelvic bones fire his cock deep into Scarlet where his hot come erupts and spreads to every nerve ending inside her. She slumps breathless onto Black's chest.

Within two hours Scarlet and her husband are showered and sitting in the office of Harry Squires, Pawnbroker.

Scarlet, Black and the second man have briefly kissed, hugged and said their goodbyes. The loan has been repaid with the agreed penalty interest.

And after they have left and as Harry sits in his office smoking his cigar and watching the film of Scarlet's violation he reflects on life as a Pawnbroker.

How Mr Kiss never needed the loan and deliberately didn't repay it. How her Honour Judge Scarlet Kiss, Chair of various women and church organisations, could live out her deepest perverted fantasies without any threat to her reputation or career. How Black the reclusive millionaire could indulge his private fantasies.

How he Harry Squires can both get a fee from each of them and sit here masturbating to the hottest film in town.

The Window Cleaner

Scarlet had enjoyed the first three months at her new house, although it would have been better still if her boyfriend had bothered to spend some time with her there as opposed to jetting off on yet more conferences on the industrial process of pizza making.

The weather had been good though for the last two weeks and she had enjoyed the seclusion her garden offered. Whilst the adjoining gardens were almost constantly filled with gaggling women and excited children she had found a spot where she could bathe naked without fear of being overlooked. The radio was playing her favourite tunes and as she sipped at her glass of red she looked at her naked body. She had never thought about her body much before but her trips to the gym were now paying off and the light tan gave her skin a healthy glow. She stretched her painted toes and admired her toned calves and thighs. She ran her nails over her pert shaven mound and shivered as her clit tingled. The breeze blew gently and made her small brown nipples hard and erect. Her finger slipped between her legs and she heard herself moan gently as she massaged herself. She much preferred cock but her boyfriend's constant travelling had long ago spelled the end to regular sex. At least his travelling had given her the time and motivation to learn about her own body. She arched her finger to ensure that she could reach her G spot then went to slip in a second.

"Hello?" came a call from the side gate

"Bugger, bugger," said Scarlet,

It was the window cleaner

Scarlet pulled her shorts on and hurriedly threw her t-shirt over her head. She scampered to the side and undid the gate.

"Hi I'm Ben. I'm standing in for Terry."

Ben was a great improvement on Terry. Nasal haired, beer bellied, chatty but slightly smelly Terry. Ben was younger, she guessed about thirty-five and black. Now Scarlet was a black virgin but had always had a secret fantasy which had tugged at her from time to time. Ben had a cute smile that made her feel naughty inside and deep brown eyes.

Her eyes wandered quickly from his face. Ben had a taut chest that stretched his t-shirt so tightly that she could see the tightness of his tummy muscles. Better still his thighs were muscular like a rugby player which enabled his toned arse cheeks to fill his jean shorts. His skin was black but glinted a petrol blue sheen as the sun caught his face.

It was clear that Ben, too, liked what he saw. Scarlet's nipples had if anything become even more erect and her still un-zipped shorts betrayed that she preferred to be bare. Scarlet quickly zipped her shorts and led Ben to the kitchen where he filled his bucket.

"I'm just going to run a bath," said Scarlet. "Is there anything I can get you a beer perhaps?"

Ben nodded to the one picture she had of her boyfriend. "I'm not sure he'll approve of me drinking his supplies."

"He won't mind. He doesn't mind sharing. Help yourself."

Scarlet made for the stairs as she heard the fridge door open behind her

There was something in what she had said which had made her unsettled but slightly aroused.

The thought rolled in her mind, like the ball on a roulette table. "Mmm. He doesn't mind sharing," what if he thought I meant me? She looked down at her erect nipples and thought again how the window cleaner must have seen at least the tip of her pussy lips.

She briefly imagined herself riding Ben pinching hard on his nipples but then let the thought drift before starting to run her bath. She entered the bedroom to undress but noticed Ben at the window. His top was off. His body was even more toned than she had imagined and she started to feel the damp spreading through her knickers. She tried hard to suppress the feeling growing inside. The one that was making her mind drift more and more towards wanting to see what this beautiful man looked like completely bare before her.

She decided to undress in the bathroom instead. Once there she pulled off her top and shorts. She heard a clang of metal on brick and Ben appeared at the window. Scarlet covered her breasts and hood with her hands but realised that Ben could barely see. The window was steaming up from the bath water.

Now this is where Scarlet should have been a good girl and dressed till Ben was finished. But Scarlet was not a good girl. Instead she went to the window and wiped the steam from two panels so that Ben could see her face.

She wrote on the next panel...? The question asked.

Ben drew a simple picture of a breast and smiled cheekily

Scarlet wiped the steam from the relevant panels so that Ben got a view of her small but perfectly formed breasts.

He breathed deep. Scarlet was well aware how wonderful her breasts were.

Again Scarlet wrote...?

Ben drew a simple cat.

Scarlet put her hand to her mouth to feign shock but then slowly and teasingly wiped the steam from the relevant panel so Ben could see her bare pussy lips in all their glory. She saw Ben look longingly and watched the bulge which had started growing steadily in his shorts.

Scarlet wrote her words – "your cock"

Ben smiled and pointed to come inside. Scarlet wagged her finger in a no, no, no sign. There, where you are she points.

Ben looked unsure. The gaggling voices coming from the adjoining gardens told him he could be seen.

"Cock," – Scarlet wrote again

Now Scarlet had a theory. A convenient theory if not one that could stand up to marital guidance scrutiny. If she never actually touched Ben and he never touched her she wasn't being unfaithful, was she?

Ben looked around to make sure it was safe then unbuttoned his jean shorts. His semi hard cock leapt forward. It was long, lean and very black with a clean pink knob. It was already wet and glistened.

"Wank." wrote Scarlet

Ben slowly worked his hands along his shaft rolling his foreskin over his knob and along his long, long shaft. Scarlet felt deliciously horny as she watched the pink of Ben's palm working his deep black shaft.

Then what she did next surprised even her

She wiped the steam so Ben could see her full body clearly. Then she started to massage her nipples with one hand and let the other fall to her clit which she started to rub in time with Ben. Ben wanked, still discreetly at first but then more urgently as his pleasure built, his eyes never leaving the sight of Scarlet now frigging her pussy. He banged his cock hard against the glass pane and pulled the skin from his foreskin as low as it would go to maximise his pleasure. Faster and faster they both wanked. Scarlet now moaning louder and louder turned on by the sight of this gorgeous man banging his perfect cock against the window for their mutual pleasure.

Knowing their orgasms were both close Scarlet knelt with her mouth touching the glass just under Ben's cock. Only the thin glass of the window separated her mouth from him. "Come for me, baby," she mouthed as she rubbed herself harder and harder.

Ben's spunk leapt from his cock onto the glass pane. Spurt after spurt. The mere sight of the spunk covered window tipped Scarlet over the edge and her own orgasm hit. Painful at first but then the waves of pleasure ran through her.

Slowly she released her fingers from her clit, lengthening and deepening the orgasm. Her body slumped whilst she captured her breath.

She looked up. Ben had gone. Disappointed she rose, slipped on her kimono and headed downstairs. He is waiting by the kitchen table.

"Now you've done your teasing girl it's my turn to play," he said.

Scarlet noticed that his cock was already hard again. Ben swept the pile of loose papers from the table then summoned Scarlet to him.

In a swift movement he lifted Scarlet onto the table

"But," she started to say.

Ben put a finger on her lips. "Shh" he said.

He spread Scarlet's legs and entered her. His cock pounding rhythmically. His full length seeming to touch the bottom of her tummy. She could feel her waves building and sobbed with pleasure.

"No, no please."

Ben smiled his body glistening with a sheen of sweat.

Scarlet's pussy muscles gripped Ben's cock as tight as they could. They were now rocking as one harder and harder till they orgasmed together, Ben filling her abused hole with the hot salty spunk he still had left in his aching balls.

They stood and kissed slowly. Both breathing deeply, each unsure how their brief liaison had come to this moment.

Finally, Scarlet reached for her purse and lazily hands Ben a £5 note.

"What's this for?"

"The windows of course."

"But they're a tenner," he quizzed.

"Yes, but have you seen the state of that bathroom window?!" she smiled.

Scarlet and the Wolves in the Wood – A fairy-tale

The steam blew from their flaring nostrils like a sinister mist that drifted across the dense wood. With barely a grunt passing between them, the three beasts continue their relentless pursuit of Scarlet.

Cursed by the King they are now half man, half wolf. Man's body, wolf's head. Charged with finding and killing Scarlet. Each know they will have her before feasting on her flesh, her scent creating rabid desires in their mutilated brains.

Scarlet knew the risk she was running. Refusing to visit the King's bedchamber was foolhardy. To decline his invitation to become Queen; a death sentence. Now as she huddled in her red cloak in the deep thicket, she gasped, waiting for breath to fill her lungs, still defiant that death was her better option. She could hear their grunts closing in on her and with what might yet be her last effort, she rips her bloomers from herself to free her legs and sprints further into the woods. She can tell from the yelps and half barks that the Wolfmen feel they are nearing the kill. It is then Scarlet stumbles and rolls. Tumbling down the small hill till she lands with a painful bump against an ancient tree root. She opens her eyes to see a small cottage. Perfectly maintained, the smoke from the chimney evidence of its occupation. Offering her only hope of survival, she beats her fists on the door and finally when there is no answer she throws herself through it and slams it shut behind her.

Her eyes are a blur as she struggles to suck in enough air to function. But then they are here. Three separate howls fill the air as they circle the cottage. Scarlet searches the cottage for a weapon, arms herself with the small chopper she finds by the fire, then waits.

The first cry of death sends a cloud of crows cawing their calls into the sky. Then a second and finally after the growl of a frightened but angry dog, a third. Then silence. Hesitantly, Scarlet opens the door. The heads of the three Wolfmen are lodged like prizes on stakes. Then he appears. The tall masked figure. Bloodied sword in hand, bloodied arms in need of attention. Unsure whether she is saved or has simply swapped one gruesome death for another, Scarlet watches on with a curious flutter of butterflies. He finally lowers his hood. His eyes sharp blue and staring. A man who wears those he has lost in his features. Once beautiful but now scarred.

And there the unlikely alliance begins. The initial hesitation. The ice broken as Scarlet takes small careful steps towards him. Approaching with the same caution she might show to a wild dog. His eyes that show the pain that might have driven others insane. Her small hand offered to him. Her hand so small against his. Leading him slowly back to the cottage before bathing his slashed and wounded arms in pure hot water. Not a wince or flicker crosses his face. They sit for some time in silence till darkness comes when he lays on the floor in front of the fire to sleep, leaving the bed for Scarlet to rest.

Scarlet watches him for a while before pulling the curtain that separates the bed from the rest of the cottage. She sleeps more soundly than she has any right to expect.

He has left the small bath filled to the brim with hot water perfumed with lavender and a tray of bread, meat and fruit. She bathes, wary of her nudity at first, but slowly relaxing in her surroundings. Not realising how hungry she is, she devours the tray of food and embarks on tidying and cleaning the cluttered cottage. By the time he returns in the late evening the cottage is transformed. Scarlett's gratitude reflected in the vases of wild flowers that perfume every room with the most delicious scent.

Still not a word spoken between them. Again he sleeps in front of the fire, but tonight thinking Scarlet is asleep, he weeps. He weeps as quietly as he can, but she hears. He weeps mourning the loss of his wife and because this is the first kindness he has been shown since she was taken from him. Briefly the anger rages through his heart but that is soon smothered and snuffed, as the loss consumes him once more. This time though it is tempered by thoughts of her, the one who bathed his arms and has already turned the cottage from a prison to a home. The one whose beautiful eyes and swirling curves conjure up deep buried sensations. His pride deserts him, as in her bare feet and full length petticoat Scarlet once again offers him her tiny hand, she leads him to the bed, then holding his head close to her breast he sleeps.

The pattern continues. Each morning he is gone by the time she awakes. Her bath poured and breakfast prepared. By the fifth morning clean clothes appear. Still each night he weeps but more gently now. And each night Scarlet rescues him from his torture and holds him tight.

His first words were said after two weeks. A simple "thank you," just before his eyes closed whilst laying in her arms. His voice a soft, gentle whisper. But then slowly there were more words, more gestures.

Scarlet just knew things had changed between them at the end of her third week at the cottage. She had returned from her walk in the woods just as the darkness of the night was closing in. The sight that greeted her made her heart flutter. The path to the cottage is lit by a mass of small oiled candles. She treads her way along the path, takes off her shoes at the door and enters. The entire floor of the cottage is decorated in flower petals such that every tread of her bare sole and toe squeezes a different perfume into the air.

Her bath is filled and readily she lets her dress slide to the floor and slips into the heat. Any tension in her muscles melts into the water as she contemplates the beauty of her new life. The beauty that brings tears to her eyes as she sees the gift he has left for her on the bed. The dress he has made entirely of fresh flowers. Gerberas entwined with lavender, daisies, spineless roses and night scented stock.

The dress fits perfectly, revealing more of her bareness than he has so far seen. By the time she hears his feet on the path, she is ready. That he thinks she is the most beautiful thing in the world, at that very moment, is reflected in his face. A face for the first time completely engaged, animated, full of lust, of want and more still. An inner delight and for the first time a smile as he looks deep inside her. This time he holds out his hand and she takes it.

She smells him. Bathed as always but also now rubbed with cones and herbs and spices. And he pulls her close into a dance and they laugh. Then they waltz and waltz some more. But that moment when they stop and their mouths are just an inch apart. Neither has kissed another out of sheer want for as long as they could remember. But now their lips do touch. At first softer than a breath then pressing harder and harder. Their mouths opening wider. Their tongues probing deeper.

She feels his fingers reach into the waist of her dress and rip it from her leaving her pussy bare. He throws her onto her back and enters her, pouring his heart and soul into her as she does him, as her ankles close and she pulls him tight into her. And then she comes. And he comes. And their cries fill the air. Longer, louder than anything they have felt before. And the crows fly higher than they ever have like a black cloud threatening rain. But nothing will affect their joy. They lay holding each other tight and then the words start to flow.

He tells how as but a boy in his early teens he had met the girl he had fallen for. A poor girl from the next village but so beautiful she would fill a man's dreams for a lifetime. How she had fallen for him and together they had built their home in the woods. How in search of wealth he had joined the King's army and rapidly risen through the ranks until he had become his most trusted bodyguard.

How the King's treacherous brother had sent him and his troop on a supposedly secret mission leaving the King unguarded. That was when the coup happened, the King was killed and the throne snatched by his loathsome brother. Worse was to follow. The new King lusted after his wife with a desire that drove him to the edge of insanity. She had been taken and held by the Wolfmen on the King's command. He and his troop so heavily outnumbered had fought till he alone stood, was then smothered and finally made to watch.

Watch whilst held clamped by the Wolfmen as the King first used, fucked and tortured his wife then killed her as she spat her contempt for him. He himself had then been beaten by the Wolves and left for dead. Delirious, wounded and near to madness he had sought salvation in the woods. And here he remained killing any Wolfmen who came near waiting for the day he could kill the King and his hated hench-Wolfman, Claw.

He had then listened in sombre silence as Scarlet had related her own story. Her story, where she had been the senior maid to a noblewoman who had been forced to audition for the King's hand. It had been plain to the Court that the King had only wanted Scarlet from the outset. To her Mistress's good fortune and Scarlet's misfortune, she had been retained in his service whilst her mistress had been banished. For weeks through guile and mischief she had managed to avoid his gruesome touch. But his short temper had finally snapped when he had forced his way into her bedchamber only to find he was forcing himself not upon her but the chambermaid with whom she had swapped chambers. Her fate was sealed when standing defiantly before him she had declined his hand.

They hold each other close, each dreaming of vengeance against the same man.

But then his disarming smile. He leaves the bed and searches a trunk she has not previously seen.

"Lay back and close your eyes," he instructs, as he lays the silk purple sheet over her.

"Are you not coming to share the bed with me?"

"Shortly, I want to watch you first."

"What are you up to?" she enquires, through accusing eyes.

It is then she feels the movement on her like tiny hands, hundreds of them alive in the sheet, stroking her, pinching her, teasing her.

"It is called the sheet of a thousand hands. It was a gift from The King of Persia for saving his son. I have many such delights to show you if you will stay."

His words trail into a mumble in her mind as the tiny hands work their magic upon her.

Tiny fingers parting her hood and holding them spread whilst yet more fingers stroke her clit through the luxuriant silk. Her bottom cheeks spread just enough for the sheet to work its way into the darkness beyond. Almost like tongues, the fingers tease the nerve endings in her puckered hole, sending shivers like small shocks through her.

The hands stroke her tummy, knead the mounds of her young pert breasts, and massage and pinch her hard pink nipples in turn. Every G spot, every nerve ending is found, used, teased and overwhelmed.

Those aching waves build deep within her, bright colours dancing through her mind. The hands know instinctively how to make her climax deeper, longer and more intense than any she has had before.

The fire rushes through her thighs and pussy, her legs shaking as her body starts to shudder and tremble.

The pictures in her mind becoming more intimate, of him fucking her, his hot white come erupting over her bright red, emerald hard clit.

Somewhere, in what she feels is probably another world, she hears herself grunt and moan as her consciousness is finally overcome by the continuous pleasure.

Finally knowing their work is done the tiny hands still and Scarlet, slumps limply against the mattress. Her blurred vision tries to focus on the ceiling. She has not seen him reach into the trunk for another treasure. He lifts the sheet from her lower body and folds his whole wet mouth around her clit and then licks softly around her rim. When he is satisfied it is sufficiently lubricated, he shows her the clock work vibrator. It has a long, slim shaft with a beautiful life-like helmet all carved from ivory.

He presses a button and three small, soft brushes flick from the lower end of the shaft. He smiles at her as he puts the key into the base and winds it like a clock.

She has barely regained her focus as the cool, hard cock slides into her soaking cunt. The effect is immediate as he slides the mechanism into action. The helmet starts to rotate and pound her. Swelling so as to first stretch her then fill her. The brushes swirling in steady circles over her clit.

She comes almost immediately. He starts to slide it from her but her hand grabs his wrist.

"No, I want more..."

The next morning Scarlet wakes alone. Her pussy still aching from her spent desires. She glides her fingertips over her bare curves as the rays of the sun cast lines across her like the aftermath of a gentle flogging. Outside the birds sing. She starts to sing along but the sensations caused by her fingers over take her and her hips buck and twitch as another orgasm pours through her. It is then she hears the first "whoosh" and another. Not bothering to cover herself she rushes to the window. He is there. Stripped to the waist. For the first time she can see his torso bared in daylight and the damage that has been done to him by the Wolfmen's claws. He holds two swords and is slowly spinning them in his wrists. The first few times one or the other is dropped. But soon she is spellbound as the speed with which he could mount an attack becomes a blur of death. It is near nightfall before he comes into the cottage his arms aching, his torso a sheen of sweat. He pulls Scarlett's head back just a little and kisses her soft beautiful mouth. His eyes now alive. A smile forms across his face as they break from their kiss.

"It's time for the King to die," he says.

The next two weeks are spent in a breathless mix of orgasms, weapon training and preparation. They settle on Scarlett's plan. Brave, foolhardy and a virtual death wish she herself describes it. He, though, just smiles at her worried frown, before sinking to his knees and, using only his tongue, slowly works her clit so her fears ease away like sweat through her pores.

She knows the night before. He has barely said a word as he sits in front of the fire and has sharpened every blade they are to carry. Her small hand reaches out to him once more and she leads him to the bed. She has stripped him, straddled him and fucked him refusing to budge from him such that for the first time he comes deep inside her.

"Tomorrow, tomorrow we will kill the King," he whispers.

The plan so very nearly works. They look like the survivors of a spent army as their silhouettes stand proud against the sun on the hill. Their horses still and calm.

The guards on duty excitedly rush to tell the other troops before word reaches Claw and then finally the King.

By the time Claw, the King and the remnants of his Wolfmen guard reach the battlements they are lined with troops. The hub bub of whispered, excited chatter quietens on their arrival.

"I thought he was dead," the King enquires nervously of Claw.

"Obviously not," Claw dryly answers, "but he soon will be."

"CLAW," Black's cry echoes its way into every corridor of the castle. "Come meet your death. Do it in glory and with what little honour you have left."

"Don't go," urges the King "I need you here to protect me."

"This is personal," Claw growls "besides what authority will you have left if I do not face him?"

Claw arms himself with his array of blades and orders the castle gate to be opened but not before he whispers his orders to the last of his kind. Four are to guard the King the other eight are to cut Black down with their bows should Claw be killed.

The battle between them is fierce and one that will be forever remembered in folklore. Each holding their duo of swords, their arms swirl in a blur of glistening metal. Each are nicked by the other, their wounds bleeding and sore, tiring their arms but knowing one mistake could cost them their life. Scarlet looks on in fear for her man, knowing also that her life depends on his.

From his place safe on the battlements, the King finally recognises Scarlet beneath her red hood. He smiles to himself planning his sexual torture of her before her death. The loathsome creature unable to resist a slow rub of his growing bulge.

The end comes with a final plunge by them both. They both howl knowing they have been hurt, but in the split second they face each other, unsure of the injuries they have inflicted on the other. It is Claw, fatally wounded who sinks to his knees then falls face first into the earth. Scarlet leaps from her horse and rushes to Black. Whilst his skin is punctured the wound has avoided artery and organ. Scarlet draws her own sword, holds it close to Black's and they kiss, as if it is their last.

The King fearful of the loss that the death of Claw will bring to his reign and incandescent with Scarlet, nods his confirmatory order to the Wolfmen that they should both be cut down with their arrows, as they enter the castle.

This is the most ambitious and speculative part of Scarlet's plan. Will the will of the people override their fear of the wicked King and his dreaded guard of Wolfmen? Perhaps buoyed by the death of Claw, the soldiers sense the changing tide. The Wolfmen now looking nervously at those they have previously tortured with fear.

"Well, what are you waiting for?" bellows the King as Scarlet and Black near the open gate?

The Wolfmen shocked back into the present draw their bows but are each ruthlessly cut down as the mutiny spreads in the ranks.

The King sensing the mutiny draws the last four Wolfmen around him in a shield, their crossbows pointing at the open gate. Black and Scarlet enter to silence, dismount and confront him.

"Drop your weapons, kneel and ask your people for their forgiveness," calls Black.

The King laughs almost exaggeratedly so. His growing insanity shining through those eyes that have lost all reason.

"Kill him," the King growls, "but save the girl, she's mine."

There is a standoff as the soldiers on the battlement all draw their bows and point their arrows of death towards the Wolfmen.

"I said kill them!" the King's voice now a squeal.

One of the Wolfmen cocks his crossbow and in that split second he and the other three Wolfmen are cut down by 100 arrows. The King picks up one of the fallen crossbows and starts to back away. Black and Scarlet slowly move forward. The soldiers all slowly edging alongside the steps in their support.

"If I'm going to die, Black, you will, too – I should have killed you when I raped your wife," the King taunts.

The bolt leaves his crossbow almost in slow motion and before the King can be cut down.

Black's life flashes through his head settling on the soft kisses he has shared with Scarlet but it never hits him. Instead Scarlet lies in a heap at his feet, she having thrown herself in its path. Black pulls his dagger from his belt and hurls it at the King. He gurgles his death rant as it severs his throat and pins him to the door behind. Black scoops Scarlet in his arms. The wound is bad. She is losing too much blood. She will die.

Die unless Black can bring himself to reveal to her and the world, the dark secret he has carried around with him since childhood and use those cursed powers to save her.

Black sees the lifeblood draining from her. That look of despair in her eyes, contemplating that their short time together is ending. Black takes the dagger from her belt and cuts a wound across his palm. He must make her like him, for her to survive. He holds his bloodied palm on her wound. Their blood starting to mingle. Slowly, very slowly her wound starts to heal. He feels that change grow within him. Like it did as a child. Powerful dark. He conveys that strength to her. Restoring her lifeless body. She must though understand the need to do what he next asks of her if she is to survive. He whispers quietly in her ear then sits on his haunches and rips his shirt from him leaving himself bare. He helps the severely weakened Scarlet to her knees, kisses her once then pulls her mouth to his neck. Instinctively like a new born baby, Scarlet knows the need to feed. The fangs now in her mouth bite a wound deep into Black's neck. Never bitten before, he knows he will severely weaken himself, maybe even die, if she is to draw enough blood to live. She drinks deeply, slowly restoring her life, slowly depleting his and that is the last both remember as they slumber into their respective comas.

It is some weeks later that the horses' clatter to the door of their cottage where they still rest and recuperate. The messenger brings news. A vote has been taken and the decision reached. The new King and Queen are to be picked on the basis of bravery, integrity and selflessness. Never again will a King or Queen be picked on bloodline alone. It is then the messenger kneels and to both of them says, "Your Royal Highnesses, I am your loyal servant."

His First Time

You wait till late before heading to bed. The lights are out at the end of the hall. Their room. The only light and sound in the house coming from the room of the other lodger. You collect your towel from your room and slide into the shared bathroom. You tense as the old iron tap creaks in its thread before the hot water oozes rather than pours into the bath. You undress then settle into the bubbles. The water slightly too hot such that it pinks your skin. And you soak. The thoughts whirl and tumble in your head. Did you misunderstand what she said? Will she really come to you? The perfume of the bath crème foaming over you, fills the room. The perfume sweet but slightly harsh as if the cleansing of your skin is a penance. You dry yourself then brush your teeth. The hall is now entirely in darkness. You can hear the fitful snoring of her husband like the far away rumble of a tube train. She must be asleep. Not sure whether to be disappointed or relieved you enter your room and flick on the bedside lamp.

You flick the switch on the record player and take an easy comfort in the whirl of the motor, the click of the needle and the scratch as the needle finds it's groove on the small cluster of 45's you have loaded.

The song, slow and melancholic makes you dwell on the love you have yet to have, the heartbreak you have yet to suffer, the sex you have yet to enjoy.

There are five records you play in all. Each with the same baleful mood. You lay there thinking of her. No longer sure if you are trying to deter her or encourage her. To keep her at distance or seduce her to your bed.

The needle clicks to the centre of the last record. You load a further small cluster but delay touching the start button. Instead you flick off your lamp and lay back covering yourself in the slightly rough blankets that prickle through the thin sheets. Your keen eyes just making out the swirling shapes of the psychedelic wallpaper in the diffused light from the lamppost outside your window. The single black and white photo on your bedside table reminding you of your real home a long way away. Of the people you have left there, of the arguments and tortures that drove you to find lodgings here in London.

Slowly your mind wanders back to her. The landlady maybe some 20 years older than your tender 17 years. The tension that has built between you. Those soft brushes from her fingers, her gentle words, the way she steps in just too close are perhaps not signals from her at all. Maybe you really have misunderstood her. The possible realisation grates deep inside your stomach. You reach for your cock under the blanket. Already hard and aching you slowly pull the foreskin down along the shaft. Your now closed eyes think of her. With her copper red curls and emerald green eyes. That soft wet mouth.

The click of a door handle turning. The door handle to her bedroom. You know it's her. She has

201

been waiting for him to fall asleep. She has lain still on her back, so as not to have ruffled her curled fringe. Waited till his soft heavy breathing has jerked and grumbled into that annoying deep, troubled snore. She has trod quietly to the wardrobe and slipped out of the nightdress she wore for him and into the sheer negligee she has saved for you. You listen as she stops and sits on the bottom step. If only you could see as she rolls the hold ups along her still shapely but pale legs.

You feel her presence now. Feigning that slow breathing that imitates sleep. Her perfume invades your senses, even through the door to your room. Deep, heavy and erotically oppressive – lily or orchid based. It floods your senses.

Her stockinged feet tip toe over the Lino. You still make out you are sleeping. So very out of your depth. Unsure if you want her to enter and take you to a world of new pleasure or to see you are asleep and leave you be. The door handle to your room is half turned but stops as she hesitates. Her dilemma – whether to open Pandora's box. Through the thin walls you hear her light a cigarette and exhale the smoke. Pacing lightly. Her decision made, the door handle is turned. You still feign sleep, ashamed of your cowardice but hoping deep inside that she will not be deterred.

She whispers your name quietly but you do not respond. She sits on the edge of the bed and you cannot resist. Your eyes open and take her in. She smiles. At that moment she is the most beautiful woman in the world. She stands and puts one foot onto the bed. Of course you are entranced. Your breath captive in your chest as if held there by this powerful wizard. She slowly slides her hold up along her smooth thighs, calf then toes. The desire to touch that bareness almost overwhelming. She slides the hold up over her fingers, then wrist, then along her arm like the glove to an evening gown then slides her fingers beneath the covers. Her silky touch stroking its way along the downy hair of your lower tummy then slowly, and shaking slightly, around your hard shaft. You cannot help the gasp you let escape in to the room as she stretches the foreskin slowly over your swollen knob, the silk of the hold-up lubricating its way along your hardness. She reaches forward and kisses your mouth so very gently. Your eyes lock with hers. The mutual look of lust, want and desire passing between you. Her mouth bites at your chin and neck then as your body is unveiled to her, your nipples and tummy.

Then her tongue cleaning the pre come from your come hole, exploring as deep as your cock will allow her entry. The sensation so delicious, you think you will come there and then and prove to be the worst ever lover but you don't. Instead you instinctively arch your back into the mattress, as her mouth and throat slowly take your full length and girth. The warm wet sensation experienced for the first time. The tongue that twirls around the sensitive filament, the teeth that grate along the length of your shaft and the lips that now suck hard on your helmet, almost trying to draw your come into her mouth.

Her stockinged fingers tighten their grip on your shaft and she starts to pump. Harder and faster whilst her mouth devours your virgin helmet. You feel the tightness in your balls, before the ecstatic rush of come along your shaft and release of tension as your come fills her mouth, then with a soft, erotic gurgle, her throat. The last eruption of your come coats hot and white against the sheer, black denier.

Her hand cups your mouth to stop your deep groan. You both giggle and kiss hard. The smell of her lipstick teasing your lips before her tongue shares your come with you.

She turns to the record player and clicks the start button. The needle teases the deck, returns to its start position then as if bored of playing hard to get, lands with a slightly bumpy crack on the groove of the record now spinning there.

The riff echoes through the room. With the benefit that only comes with youth you need no recovery time. She straddles you with her thighs and strokes your cock around her sopping wet slit before your virginity is lost forever. Lost as her soft wet velvet glove-like pussy slides over your hard curved cock. You gasp together. She pauses just for a single moment then slowly starts to rock then buck along you as if you are a wild horse being broken.

Your hands instinctively reach under her negligee and explore her wide womanly hips, her softer full tummy and her firm heavy breasts. Kneading them gently as you feel her nipples harden under your palms.

You cannot believe you are fucking this Goddess. Cannot believe she wants you.

She leans forward and you kiss again. Her hot mouth touching yours, she takes her mouth away as your tongue tries to probe her.

"Tut, tut," she teases.

You learn quickly. This time as her mouth touches yours your tongue stays still. You listen as her filthy mouth talks to yours, her words drifting through the back of your throat to your brain.

Her cunt now clenching tightly around your shaft. She rises slightly and pinches hard on both nipples, turning and twisting them as if steering you like a human control panel.

"Come for me, baby," she breathes "come inside me. Fill me with your young hot come."

Your hips now fire your cock into her like a jackhammer.

"Oh yes, yes, just like that."

And you do, even as your hot come floods into her, your hips fire against her, and you see the first orgasm you have ever given to a woman, as she growls then moans her pleasure even over the music.

It is your turn to cover her mouth with your hand. You wince as she bites it to suppress the waves flooding through her.

Slowly her heaving chest stills, her eyes open and she smiles.

"Clean me, baby."

She works her thighs along your chest and shoulders until her pussy straddles your mouth.

"Clean me softly."

She lowers her cunt onto your mouth. The strong salty acidic spunk mixed with her beautiful musky come. The thought of you licking and sucking on your own come seems so wrong but feels so right as you feel her grinding on your tongue.

Faster and faster your tongue flicks against her, responding to the purring moans. The come leaking from her coating your throat as it slides on its way to your stomach. And she shudders as she comes again. You cannot breathe as her pussy collapses over your mouth. It is only as she jerks your hair back that you finally gulp in the air.

"I have to go," she says

"Stay," you plead.

"You know I can't, I will come again soon. Saturday," He is out Saturday. "Don't look so sad."

You smile back at her as she kisses you one last time before she is gone.

You stay awake long into the night celebrating the loss of your virginity and re-living every beautiful moment. The thought of her adultery does not cross your mind, until you see him at breakfast. He enters from behind you just as she leaves your breakfast on the table.

Still standing before you, he looks at your breakfast.

"You have an extra sausage. I thought as much."

Your brain struggles to form a response but he saves you the trouble.

"I like it, just make sure you tell me every detail."

Your black pudding refuses to be swallowed as your eyes settle on the bulge forming in the front of his trousers.

Her First Time

I try so hard to be a good wife.

I shop, I cook, I clean, I wash and I sink to my knees more than most girls I know.

But I married young, before I really understood all the pleasures there were to be had. Tom is a good man, a fine man. Handsome to most, charming to all. He still is to me, but I am bored. I am loved admired and trapped. I want some freedom.

I have dark thoughts. I see older men as I walk through the High Court where I work. I see their crisp suits and dark polished brogues. I smell their cologne and like their smart sophisticated chatter. I imagine being called to their Chambers where I am humiliated then spanked over their knee, my wet knickers left like handkerchiefs in their lapels.

But then I like the mucky boys, too. The car mechanics.

I see them locking the doors to their dirty dark garage with me still inside when I cannot pay the bill. Forcing me to my knees, sucking them all until I cannot swallow any more.

I have looked very briefly at sex sites and clubs, but it's all so difficult.

I recently watched a documentary on TV when Tom was sleeping on the sofa. A programme about swingers. A young woman, her face blurred to protect her identity, gives me the final piece of my puzzle. She is asked how she hides her guilt from her non-swinger husband.

"I have a character – Pandora. It is she who plays not me. When I have finished at an event Pandora goes into her box and I become me again. No one knows. No one needs to know."

This took some days to reconcile in my head. I felt awful every time I looked at Tom, knowing what I was possibly about to do.

I waited until it was Tom's five-a-side football night. I sat on my computer and googled the key words I thought might identify the site I might most like to join. I sat mouth agape as rows and rows of cock pictures filled my screen. Slowly my head stopped spinning and I got to work. By the time Tom had returned and showered, I had formed a new email account and had posted a basic profile. The next day I uploaded a picture of my long legs dressed in the highest heels that I own with my ankles tied together with a stocking.

I was overwhelmed with messages. Okay some were basic, "Come fuck me bitch" type messages and some were just pictures – it took me some time to tire of those. But amongst them all were offers that drove my imagination wild.

The problem for me though was getting the nerve to actually do anything in person as opposed to simply talking about it in in my messages.

I talked dirty. I seduced them, aroused them and told them all of the perverted things I would do when we met in person, but I never confirmed a meet. Well not until I heard from Mr and Mrs Smith. They made me feel relaxed and confident. I told them I wasn't sure I could actually join in. They said they understood.

They booked a table for us to meet in a basement wine bar. It turned out that it was a table for one. My drink was pre ordered and I sat on my barstool. I looked around at the other customers wondering which of them were Mr and Mrs Smith. The text pinged into my phone.

"Look out the window."

Above me at ground level, I saw first her heels, then her long stockinged legs. I guessed it was an alleyway that ran alongside the wine bar. It was dark and her image was like a grainy black and white movie filmed under the diffused light of the lamppost.

I saw the hands behind her lift her skirt and slide her knickers to her ankles.

It was like watching a show in a theatre for one. My pussy clenched as I saw his hands unclip each stocking from the suspender belt in turn and roll it down each long smooth moisturised leg.

And then he fucked her. From behind. I watched as he stretched her then slowly drove his cock in and out. Nearly bent in two, I could not see her face, but watched as one hand reached between her legs and rubbed her bare shaven clit. I could hear her pant. I heard her moan as she came.

My straw sucked on fresh air and ice so taken was I with the show.

And then Mrs Smith sank to her knees. She was beautiful. Dark hair, green eyes, pale freckled skin. Her bareness fully on display. There were three men at first. Three cocks. Taking one each in turn, her saliva making each glisten. She caught my eye, winked softly and beckoned me to join.

My mind raced, I looked around at the other customers sure that each and every one of them was staring at me, judging me.

But then I turned back to Mrs Smith, her cheek stretched and distorted by the huge cock between her lips. I should have just left and gone home. But I knew I wouldn't; I left the bar and walked around the dark car park where I found the person-sized hole in the chicken wire. I heard them before I saw them.

Four men now surrounding this beautiful creature on her knees.

"Mrs Smith?" my voice trembled.

"Thank God for the fucking cavalry, Scarlet," she purred back.

The first man kissed me before I could run. He was beautiful. Old but smelled clean and sharp. Just like at the Court. His tongue delved deep into my throat. I couldn't breathe but I loved it.

He placed my hand on his bare hard stubby cock. Only the fourth cock I had ever touched in my life. I grip it tightly and stroke the foreskin over his wet helmet. I feel hands behind me, lifting my skirt. I don't resist as his cool fingers slide between my skin and the silk and slide my knickers down my bare legs.

His hands grab a fistful of my hair and he turns me. His tongue now penetrates my lips. The first man's hands are surging under my top. His strong lean and long fingers slide under my bra and knead the mounds of my breasts. I can feel my love juice leaking from my pussy. My hands reach for the second cock. Instinctively I join their come holes, so their helmets each soaking wet in their pre come are rubbing against each other. Slowly wanking their foreskins so my fists bump into each other. I can hear their pleasure. The – for me – surreal pleasure of a man other than Tom, growling and telling me he wants to fuck me.

And then I feel the gentle pressure of a hand on my shoulder forcing me onto all fours. Mrs Smith is already there. She briefly kisses me then opens her mouth to await her gift.

And we are both spit roasted, like sensual erotic meat. My mouth folded around the older man, the second filling my aching pussy from behind.

My sensibilities are lost. There is no risk assessment. There are no consequences. All I feel is lust. I want to be fucked. I want to be their come bucket. His pelvic bone slaps into my arse cheeks. My mind works to the rhythm of our flesh clashing. I hear the betraying grunt from the man in front. The grunt that tells me his come will soon force its way through his helmet deep into my throat. I don't always swallow Tom but today I want it all.

I am a slut. A whore. And I love it.

I gag a little as he pours into me. Filling my throat so I have to adjust and breathe before I can swallow his second load. It's delicious like his cologne has flavoured his salty gift.

As he stands back from me I find myself face to face with Mrs Smith. As we both rock forward her long cat like tongue cleans my mouth of the spilled come.

It's all too much for me and I come deep and hard, my pussy muscles gripping on the shaft within me.

And he pulls out just in time, holding his helmet tight against my anus and letting it erupt there. My mind pictures that hot white come against my small black puckered hole.

We rest and pant until we catch our breaths. We are helped to our feet and kissed and hugged. The belated introductions are brief. Each of us has a user name.

Mr and Mrs Smith walk me to my car. The conversation is easy. They tell me of their next planned event. I want to go.

It is as I am finally left alone that I fear the guilt will hit me. My adultery. My infidelity.

But it doesn't not for one moment. Scarlet and her wardrobe are mid-wash in the washing machine as Tom comes home late. I greet him with a glass of white wine and a ready smile.

"Good day, love?" he asks.

"Yes, okay, Tom," I lie, "Not bad at all."

The Burglary

The plan had all seemed so simple soaking in the bath the night before. She had smiled as she stretched her toes in the bubbles and had slipped back into the hot perfumed water.

Dan, her no good ex, had promised her 100 times that he would repay her the £5,000 she was due from the joint account but here she was five months later and still waiting. Business is bad, the tax needs paying, I have to go see "some people," to see if I can borrow it... Scarlet had heard all the excuses. The truth was this was small change to Dan.

She had pondered long and hard before the "light bulb," above her head shone bright and she had remembered that he used to keep his cash float from his restaurant in the safe at his flat. She had bet herself that he still kept the spare key under the flowerpot on the back step. He would never think to change the combination either. It would be simple to gain entry, raid the safe and take the money and leave him a little thank you note. The smile spread across her face as she thought of Dan's furious face as he opened the safe and found her thank you note scrawled across the back of his favourite tight boxers.

So this is how Scarlet came to be on the back step of the flat she had shared with Dan the previous year.

She had ridden there on her motorbike and parked it a little along the road in case Dan was home and had recognised the engine noise. She undid the zip on her black leathers to mid chest to let in some air, tied a scarf around her mouth and nose as a disguise and pulled her hair tight back.

She caught her reflection in the glass of the back door and it made her jump. But then she looked closer. Scarlet had always been kept in the shadows by Dan but these months of freedom had really opened her world and she liked what she saw.

Her eyes dazzled in the glass and the scarf made her look dark and mysterious. The streetlight caught the top of her breasts and cleavage and made them glow. She undid the zip a little more and felt a warm glow in her pussy as she purred at the effect.

As predicted the key was still under the flower pot and she silently let herself into the kitchen. Same old Dan she thought. The kitchen was a mess. Pans and plates littered the sink and odd items of clothing were left lying around like the bodies had been mysteriously sucked from them. The hall was clear and she headed towards the bedroom where she knew the safe could be found. The bedroom door was ajar and she peered in. The moonlight filtered through the net curtains onto the bed. Only a naked foot appeared from under the quilt and the gentle snoring told Scarlet the coast was clear.

She tiptoed to the wardrobe and soon found the safe. Dan had no idea Scarlet knew the combination. That she had found on his mobile whilst she had been checking for texts from his mistress.

5,7,4,2,1

The door slowly swung open. Scarlet smiled. Mmmm. There was cash but not as much as she had expected. Maybe £2,000 but there was some nice jewellery and a Rolex. So the sly old dog had been doing better than he had let on. Well Rolex and jewellery you are now kidnapped until he pays the ransom she thought. Scarlet put the cash and jewellery down her top, closed the safe door and quietly slipped across the bedroom floor.

The figure in the bed stirred and she stood still holding her breath.

She and Dan had ended on okay terms and talked on and off but he was likely to have one of his explosive temper tantrums if he caught her now.

The figure stilled and Scarlet turned to leave. Her heart froze though as a hand suddenly reached in from the hall and flicked on the light switch. The door was pushed open.

"Oh shit," whispered Scarlet to herself. This wasn't Dan. This certainly wasn't Dan. If she hadn't been in such trouble she would have most certainly appreciated the eye candy now standing in front of her. The stranger had dark cropped hair and smouldering brown eyes. He wore a small vest through which his chest muscles stretched. His biceps and triceps competed with each other for attention.

The stranger pulled something from his pocket and with a flick of his wrist a blade appeared.

"Hey, honey, we have a guest," he called to the figure in the bed.

The covers are hurriedly thrown back and a naked woman slips from the sheets.

"Who are you?" the woman shouts genuinely startled.

"Where is Dan?" asks Scarlet nervously through the mask.

"Who?" said stranger.

"Dan...this is his flat."

"Never heard of the fella but nice try Sugar."

"He was my ex he lives here."

"Not very close then are you? We've been renting this place from the agency for two months."

"Shall I ring the Police?" Asks the woman pulling a kimono around her slim frame.

The pause hangs heavy in the air.

"Mmm. Let me think. Sit on the bed," he orders Scarlet

The stranger and the woman whisper to each other for what seems like forever whilst a now petrified and remorseful Scarlet looks on. A knowing and cruel smile suddenly passes across the man's lips.

"Come with me," he orders.

At knife point Scarlet is led to the lounge and the lights switched on. The room has been turned into what looks like a photographic studio. There are cameras and video cameras parked on each wall interspersed with professional lighting. The floor, ceiling and each wall house a large screen.

"What are you doing?" asks Scarlet her fear evident in her trembling voice.

"What are we doing? I don't suppose you want to tell us what you were doing?"

"Dan owes me money. I came to get it back."

"You're a common thief," accuses the stranger. "I should call the police now."

"No please don't" begs Scarlet, the full horror of her situation starting to sink in.

The Rolex nestling against her nipples, a very obvious physical reminder.

"So what do you think?" The stranger says to the woman, "Will she go to prison? The girls there will just love her!"

Scarlet looks at the woman properly for the first time. She is tall, nearly six foot, slim with cropped fringeless blonde hair to match stranger's. The hairline beautifully showing off her shining blue eyes and soft pouting lips.

"By the time you tell the police that you had to take that knife off her then it's certainly prison," the blond woman teases coldly.

"But I didn't' have the... knife (pause),"

Scarlet knew then she was done for. She is entirely at the mercy of this man and woman. Only they know what they have planned for her.

"Take off the mask," orders the stranger.

Scarlet does as she is told and even in her darkest hour is pleased to see stranger's reaction.

"Very nice," he said "cute."

The woman gently pads around the room barefoot clicking at the buttons of a remote control and soon the room is humming with the sound of equipment readying itself for use.

The man raises the blade, "My watch and money please."

Scarlet reaches inside her leathers.

"Ah no," the stranger says, "undo the zip."

The screens briefly flash blue and then Scarlet's image lights up each screen. She is to be filmed.

She lowers the zip slowly till the tip of the watch is visible.

"Keep going," stranger prompts

Scarlet lowers the zip till it reaches the tip of her pussy lips.

"Now slide your leathers from your shoulders."

"But I'm naked underneath," protests Scarlet

"So," says the stranger cruelly.

Scarlet slips the leathers slowly to her waist. The woman strokes her long nails down Scarlet's spine exhaling a little purr. It makes every one of Scarlet's nerve ends tingle. The stranger collects the Rolex from the ruffled up waistline but lets the money and jewellery fall like snow to the floor.

"So, honey, what do we think of our new star?" he asks.

The woman stands aside Scarlet to admire her perfectly formed breasts.

"Is someone enjoying this naughty girl?" She asks as she brushes her nails over Scarlet's already stiffening deep brown nipples.

"I don't know what your game is..." snaps Scarlet

"Shhh," says woman and she surprises Scarlet with a soft honey flavoured kiss.

"What the fuck are you doing," growls Scarlet – although in truth the kiss arouses her and her moistening pussy lips start to betray her.

"I really don't think our little burglar knows quite how much trouble she is in," whispers stranger. The pause hangs long in the air.

The woman edges closer and closer to Scarlet. Scarlet's heart pounds in anticipation. The same honey flavoured breath and their lips touch.

Scarlet feels the woman's probing tongue enter her mouth. Almost involuntarily Scarlet finds her mouth opening to receive the woman. Scarlet has never kissed a woman before. This is her virgin kiss and she likes it. More gentle than any man she has known, a feeling deep inside that her tongue is being slowly seduced. She gasps slightly as the woman pinches her nipple. Suddenly the woman breaks the kiss and takes two steps back.

"Now the rest," orders the man

Scarlet's head is starting to spin and her throat feels dry. Only Dan has seen her naked these last few years and here she is being forced to strip in front of strangers.

"No I won't – that's too far," she retorts

"Sure?" asks stranger.

"No I won't," says Scarlet suddenly slightly less sure.

"That's fine," says the stranger.

He reaches for his mobile phone and dials 999... "Are you really sure?" he asks.

"Yes," Scarlet gulps, the butterflies in her tummy telling her just how badly she has misjudged this situation.

"Okay," he smiles.

He clicks the phone on to loud speaker. Scarlet can hear it ring. The phone is answered,

"Police, fire or ambulance what service do you require?"

"Okay," Scarlet cracks "anything."

Stranger clicks the cancel button on the phone and the call is disconnected.

"Now I have your attention finally. We will not hurt you as long as you do all that we say. But you must do everything. Okay?"

"Okay, deal," says Scarlet in a very quiet sombre voice.

She pulls the boots from her feet and slides the leathers from her, leaving her bare.

The woman feels her tight, toned bum cheeks and growls slightly as she sees Scarlet's newly shaven mound, which is already showing signs of excitement.

"Mmm. You're perfect."

The stranger walks to a small sink in the corner and pours a bowl of water which he places before Scarlet. He slides off his vest. Scarlet can feel her juices stirring within her. The involuntary lust now ignited as she resigns herself to their punishment.

She feels her mouth open slightly as his muscles ripple. He slides his jeans to the floor leaving him only in tight boxers. Scarlet can see the length of his shaft pushing tightly against the material and the very tip of his swollen knob poking through the band at the top.

The woman appears behind him and teasingly pulls the boxers down to reveal his mighty cock inch by slow inch.

"Kneel," he says

Scarlet kneels obediently, her mind screaming at her to run for safety but her desire to be now taken by this couple taking over. The strangers cock is no more than a foot away. Again her mouth involuntarily opens as she feels the urge to suck him hard.

"Wash me," he commands.

At the woman's prompting, Scarlet reaches for the bowl and builds a small lather of soap which she massages into his cock. Her bathing makes him hard. Rock hard. The hardest and stiffest she has ever felt any man.

"Now rinse."

Scarlet uses her cupped hands to pour the clean water over him, slowly rolling back his foreskin before pouring more water over that sensitive skin.

"Now come suck me."

The woman joins Scarlet on her knees and kisses her again

"You first," she prompts.

Scarlet takes the strangers helmet into her mouth, just into that small area behind her lips. The salty leak wakes her taste buds, the smell of soap drifting into her nose.

"Hey greedy," says the woman "I want some too."

Scarlet lets him go and the woman leans over to kiss her with stranger's cock trapped in between. Their tongues dancing, each flicking the big purple helmet standing hard between them. Scarlet notices the action is being projected onto every screen from every angle. Feeling so wet and horny now. The mixture of enforcement, humiliation and filming and the soft kisses make her reach between her own legs. Her fingers pressing hard against her swollen clit.

"Tut tut, who said you could pleasure yourself?" admonishes the stranger. "On all fours," he commands. "I think you need to learn some patience."

The stranger stands in front of her, his cock at the same level as her mouth but slightly out of reach.

Scarlet feels warm oil being poured over her bum cheeks and pussy by the woman. The woman's hands starting to work at her clit. Slowly massaging in firm slow circles. Scarlet feels a finger circling her puckered hole. Then a soft kiss placed on it followed by a gently probing tongue. The tongue works in the same steady rhythm as the fingers. The woman purrs

"Mmm. What a delicious little arse you have, my darling."

Scarlet feels her waves building, she tries desperately to reach stranger's cock but he keeps it just from her reach. Every screen now shows her shiny arse with the beautiful woman's head bobbing in and out. Then from below her pussy lips and red swollen abused clit covered in oil being tortured by the woman's fingers.

"I'm coming. No, no, no," Scarlet shouts having no control over the pleasure forced upon her or the timing of her climax. The words bounce around the room on surround sound. The pleasure and pain run through her like a tsunami and she slumps on her chest with her bum in the air and her legs trembling. Scarlet opens her eyes to see her own face stare back at her on the screen. The serenity of her orgasm, her face coated in a slight sheen of perspiration.

"Thank you for getting her ready honey," says the stranger as he settles behind Scarlet. He enters her hard and fast. Pulling her hair so hard her head jerks back hard. Scarlet tries to rise but cannot as the still, hard, very hard cock pummels her already aching hole. Every inch sliding in, then out. The swollen helmet stretching the entrance before the long shaft fills her cavity. Scarlet can feel his balls slapping her, each time tightening just a little more.

The screens now show only two things, Scarlet's serene face as her second orgasm builds within her and the sight of the stranger's cock and balls abusing her red violated cunt.

Scarlet comes first, wave after wave, like an earthquake of heat searing through her clit and cunt. Her long banshee scream filling her head, sharing space with those intense colours of orange and purple that flash through her brain.

The stranger twitches and jerks.

Scarlet feels his hot sticky load fill her as he groans and pulls her pussy tight to his pelvic bone.

It is a minute or so later that he finally takes his still semi hard cock from her.

Exhausted Scarlet smiles. The screens now focusing just on her cunt as the come leaks then drips lazily onto the lens below.

The night continues at pace and it is a happy tired but sore Scarlet who leaves the flat at 3 a.m. As she opens her front door she slips on an envelope which has been pushed through the letterbox. It is Dan's writing.

Scarlet does not know whether to laugh or cry as she looks at the cheque for £5,000 and the note inside which says:

"Hi, Scarlet, sorry for the delay but here's the money I owe you. Ps. Note my new address. Love Dan."

He Should Never Have Laughed

"He should never have laughed," growled Scarlet menacingly as she recalled that day.

That day when they had inflicted their awful punishment on her for the theft of one loaf of bread. The loaf of bread that might have saved her siblings from a life of prostitution or worse.

She slid her hand through her blouse and let the tips of her fingers glide over the scars that they had left.

He had seen her withdraw into herself almost every day since and knew well enough to keep his silence until she returned to him, this beautiful scarred, once nearly broken Scarlet.

Her eyes flared as she thought back to that day. As she recalled being led from the stinking cells of Newgate prison and through the baying crowd hurling abuse at her for sport.

How her starving body had been tied to the whipping post and her blouse ripped from her. Her breasts laid bare for the lusting eyes of the beckoning crowd ready to fuck her defenceless bones if she was ever to survive this torture and be cut free.

Their eyes had taken in her taut brown nipples and pert mounds. Men freely reaching for the cocks hardening in their breeches.

She told herself she would show no fear and she didn't, not even as the first lash from the cat's tail cut through her skin and she felt the first drop of her blood drip onto her stomach.

She had dug her nails deep into her palm until the sting had passed and that deep heat raced through her.

Knowing the only way she would survive was to turn the pain into pleasure, her mind had started to beckon the next lash, the next sting. Digging her nails ever deeper into her palms until they looked like she had been crucified.

The darkness, though, slowly overtook even her. Her weakened body taking ever longer to recover from each blow. She had seen those in the crowd openly ejaculating as they climaxed to her inhumane punishment. She had closed her eyes believing the end neared for her.

The pain and heckling now one humming blur she had blacked out slumped against the post. She had vaguely sensed being untied but it was the icy cold water that stung her body and moistened her mouth that give her the chance of what she thought was one last look at the sorry stench of her world.

It was the crows that had first circled, then pecked at her open wounds that had made her look up. Look at him. He had laughed as one particularly ambitious crow had torn a tear of flesh from just above her still bare nipple.

Him, Frederick the womanising heir to the King of this God-forsaken country that had abandoned its poor and needy. Him, the Dandy, with his prematurely aged and bloated face, distorted by the feasts at Court that had fed a mere 20 guests when there was enough to feed 200.

She would never forget or forgive his laughter.

How the stranger, Black, had saved her she still did not know.

She had woken on his bed in a howl of pain. Initially holding him at bay for some twenty minutes with his knife, he had gently and softly soothed her fears. Cautiously she had finally lowered the knife and allowed him to take her hand and lead her to the adjoining room.

Once there he had removed the silk cloak he had placed around her to restore her modesty and started to bathe and cleanse her wheals and the open wounds that latticed across her breasts, stomach and hips.

A strange erotic yet still uneasy alliance had unfolded as she sat bare before this stranger whilst he had first sterilised the needle by flame then pierced it through her skin to stitch the worst of her wounds.

The brandy she swigged at freely, barely numbed each puncture of her skin. The cigar she drew on blew a hazy perfumed mist between them.

As she did when tied to the post, Scarlet turned that pain into her pleasure, her mind now making Black her torturer, her lover.

Black for his part had fallen deeply for the beautiful creature before him. Unsure how to reconcile within himself the stiffening of his cock with each stitch he placed in Scarlet's skin.

Their depraved pleasures understood by each of them without a word passing from their lips.

Scarlet smiling for the first time for as long as she could remember as she saw the twisted pleasure in his face first as he punctured her skin then as she stubbed her cigar on his bare chest.

Relighting the cigar, this twisted foreplay unfolded between them. For every third stitch she would delight in the all too brief sizzle as the tip of her cigar tortured his muscular torso.

Then finally the pause as he pulled the needle through the wound just above her bare nipple and cut the thread for one last time. Cut that thread just as she stubbed that cigar to its butt on his bare, taut shoulder.

And as if close to their respective climax, they had looked into each other's eyes. Breathless and near physically spent, she had noticed the outline of Black's cock pressing hard against the outline of his breeches as he had risen and gathered the small cluster of lit candles onto the table between them.

She could feel her own juices seeping into the crotch of her breeches, that soft musky smell slowly filling the air between them.

Black had never forgotten that look in her eyes as he had risen before her. She wanting, needing what he was about to do. Pleading, vulnerable, but defiant as he had tipped the hot molten wax over each of the stitches to seal them and to protect her from infection.

Her cry had filled the room but it had not been a cry of pain. No this was a cry of pleasure. A cry soft and melodic, as her orgasm overtook not only her body but her very soul and being.

Still shuddering in her aftershocks Black had lifted her into his arms and lain her gently on his bed. She had turned her head to face the wall and watched as his silhouette had removed her boots and then her breaches leaving her entirely naked before him.

Tingles had flooded her body like tiny shocks first as she had watched his silhouette strip bare then sink to its knees and let its mouth gently kiss her reddening swollen hood. His mouth had sensed her every want, her every pleasure, just as if it had been her own mouth pleasuring her.

Letting his tongue draw over her hood like loose fine silk Black was in no hurry. From the base of Scarlet's tight cunt to the tip of the skin protecting her clit like armour, Black let his tongue drift. Feeling her thighs tremor, her stomach clench, her breathing become more shallow. Scarlet now willing that tongue to split her hood, and it finally does.

Scarlet watches the silhouette as its head rocks between her spread thighs. Feeling the deep throb as Black's mouth sucks in the small inner hood and draws her tight hard clit into his mouth. Almost as soft as air the tip of his tongue rolls around her clit.

She hears her own murmur as Black's long middle finger strokes the rim of her cunt before it slides through into the sticky hot wetness beyond. Her murmur becomes a long slow moan as a second and third finger start to stretch and fill her whilst that tongue still works its steady, slow soft magic.

His fingers, glistening in her juices, slide in and out from fingertips to knuckle like an unrelenting, impossible to satiate cock. Her cunt, seduced and overwhelmed, rocks in rhythm and still that relentless mouth flicks, massages, sucks and bites at that ruby hard clit.

Almost as if back tied to the whipping post, the relentless torture takes its toll. The waves build deep in her thighs, deep in her stomach. The thoughts in her head become ever more depraved as her orgasm nears.

Her final thought is of them both bare, Black fucking her hard against the post whilst they are both whipped by a dozen hands, and with the Prince rocking back in his throne laughing.

Even as her orgasm rocks her thin body, her brain nags in its menace... "he should never have laughed."

That was two years ago and in the intervening time Black and Scarlet had become the most infamous of highwaymen.

Always targeting the Prince's coaches or those of his known allies and courtiers they had made themselves a fortune upon which they could have retired to a privileged and wealthy life. But that is not what had driven them. No it was the delight they took in the Prince's growing fury and his ever more desperate attempts to capture them.

This night they had eaten well and had fucked even better. It was as they lay in bed sipping at the Port they had seized on their last raid that their conversation had drifted from mischievous frivolity to disturbed chatter.

They rarely disagreed on targets. It was even more rare for them to argue between themselves, but this was one such time.

"Scarlet, this is madness," exclaimed Black,

"He shouldn't have laughed."

"Of course he shouldn't but this will see us hung, drawn and quartered for sure."

"You're scared?" she mocks

"Of nothing. Of fucking nothing, but we will never be let one moment's rest if we attempt this."

"Do you really believe we will find each other in the next life, if we are caught and killed? Do you really believe our souls are so entwined that whoever we are, whatever we are we will find each other?"

"Of that I am certain, Scarlet."

"Then the worst that happens is only one of us dies."

And so the decision was made.

Despite the heavy taxes imposed by Parliament newspapers continued to flourish in popularity. It was the *Daily Courant*, that reported on the intention to move the Crown Jewels from the Jewel House at the Tower of London to Warwick Castle.

With the announcement came the anticipated kettling of thieves, rogues, mercenaries and Celts into Newgate. Scarlet and Black sit in their favourite hide, just watching. Spies, spies everywhere promising riches, threatening death. Calling in favours and promises. And they watch and watch and listen soaking up every rumour, every piece of information they can until the day finally arrives.

The train put together to escort the Crown Jewels, was impressive by any standard. Fifteen pristine coaches with armed lookouts sitting both at the front and rear of each carriage flanked by two hundred, heavily armed cavalry.

Slowly, so slowly it made its way from the Tower through the streets of London before finding the open spaces of Finchley Common.

And yet hidden away in the woods are Scarlet and Black. Their horses breathing steam into the chilled autumnal air. Each nervously checking their pistols. It was as the first of the horses clopped at pace on the highway below that they pulled their masks to their faces and charged.

The Prince and the Crown jewels arrive safely in Warwick Castle. The Prince smiles just a little too smugly as he looks at his reflection in the base of his empty, silver goblet. He takes in the merriment of his fat Court as they chatter and laugh in a confetti of thrown chewed and spent bird bones and slurp too quickly on endless jugs of fine wine.

It is only as he drains his newly filled goblet that he sees the courier waiting nervously at the door to the dining hall.

The dining room is brought to immediate silence by the clap of his hand. The blood that turns his face from its usually flushed pink, to its furious red, in turn sends his clenched knuckles to a drained white.

You see the Crown Jewels are not his to lose, they belong to the Country. But his own Crown Jewel, his finance, Princess Augusta is his to lose. And lose her he has.

The first two pistol shots take out the driver and his guard. The second two shots take out the front escort. By the time Scarlet has her sword through the heart of the only cavalryman brave enough to stand his ground the panic sets in and the remaining escort retreats to the safety of the road they have just travelled from.

"Princess Augusta?" welcomes Scarlet.

There is much to admire of Princess Augusta with her beautiful saucer wide green eyes, rose coloured full lips and her refusal to wear the wig of the Court in favour of her natural auburn hair. More still is the lack of drama, the lack of histrionics. She is their prisoner. A ransom will undoubtedly need to be paid.

Before the carriage is abandoned, the Princess is forced to change into riding clothes in the carriage and having rounded up the horse of one of the dead soldiers the three ride into the woods...

In the lodge hidden deep within the woods, the Princess is led to the largest chair in front of the fire where her wrists are tied to each arm.

Black rests in a chair whilst Scarlet paces the floor. They watch her as like a pendulum she swings from one side of the room to the other. She pours a brandy and holds it to the Princess's lips.

"Drink."

"It is too early for me thank you."

"Trust me – drink, you'll need it."

Uncertain of what is to follow but heedful of the warning Princess Augusta allows Scarlet to tip the full goblet into her open mouth. The brandy burns like fire water as it traces its path to her stomach. She gasps to let in air.

Scarlet kneels before her and watches until she can tell from Augusta's eyes that the alcohol has started to numb her senses.

She smiles at Augusta softly, removes her boot from her otherwise bare right foot, briefly sterilises the blade of her knife over a candle and slices a deep cut in her sole.

Notwithstanding the sense numbing brandy Augusta's scream fills the lodge.

"Just like a girl," bemoans Scarlet dismissively.

Holding that bleeding foot tightly in her hands, Scarlet lowers her mouth and slowly licks the full length of the wound with her soft wet tongue. Black and Scarlet each notice that flicker in Augusta's eyes.

The same flicker that appeared in theirs that first night together.

Once more Scarlet's mouth teases the wound and again that flicker in Augusta's eyes.

Scarlet reaches for the nearest candle and tips the molten wax over the wound.

"That will seal the wound, you will walk freely indoors and we will not tie you. Try to escape and the earth will rip open and infect the wound. Your choice."

With that Scarlet cuts Augusta's wrists free of their restrains and pours brandies for them all.

They sit still and in silence for the next hour. It is only as the fire starts to burn down and the night falls that Black rises and puts more logs on the dimming fire and lights more candles. He pours three more brandies and again they sit.

It is Scarlet who finally cuts through the silence.

"Are you not wondering why you have been taken?"

"I am Prince Frederick's fiancée; I presume that is why you have chosen me. I am sure he will pay a handsome reward for my return."

"That is indeed partly why you have been chosen. He is said to love you very much...but it is not for ransom."

"No ransom?" Then what do you want from me or him?"

"Your pain and his shame."

"I don't understand..."

"Stand up."

Augusta does as she is commanded and winces slightly as her weight steps on her sealed wound. Scarlet slowly unbuttons the cuffs of her own blouse, then the buttons along its front and lets it fall to the ground. A look of horror and bemused lust spreads across Augusta's face as she looks at the criss-cross of scars that line Scarlets breasts and torso.

Scarlet reaches out for Augusta's hands. Once in hers she places them on her beasts.

"Feel the wounds, the scars, ones that no woman should ever be marked by."

Almost childlike Augusta traces her finger along the length of the scars, across Scarlet's breasts, nipples, tummy and sharp hips.

Her features betraying not disgust or repugnance or pity but a frisson of jealous want.

"You know why and how I came by these?"

"No...tell me."

"I stole a simple loaf of bread to feed my orphaned sisters. I was caught and held in Newgate. I had to let the Judge fuck me to avoid the noose and the warder fuck me so I had food enough to make the flogging. I was dragged to the platform where I was stripped to the waist, my breasts bare for the perverted mob to feast their filthy minds on. And then they flogged me raw. I lost count of the blows. Lost any sense of humanity as my flesh was torn from me by that leather with the crowd baying. And then they let the crows feed on me and do you know the thing I remember above all else."

"No?"

"Your fiancé, the bloated pig Frederick, laughing as the crows tore at me."

Augusta's hands reach back to Scarlet's breasts and tummy lightly stroking the scars.

"And so my Princess I made myself a promise that one day somehow I would get my revenge. And sadly for you today is that day."

Scarlet advances towards Augusta her sheer presence making the younger woman retreat. Retreat until she backs into the big oak beam shoring the roof.

"Give me your hands...now."

Black, his cigar smoke curling across the room, has watched on becoming ever more aroused at this depraved dynamic. From the small trace of blood left by Augusta's bleeding sole as she retreats, to that look of wonderment on her face as she too slowly and carefully stroked at Scarlet's scarred breasts, to Scarlet's small, involuntary gasp as she did so and as Augusta too compliantly, too willingly surrenders to her fate.

Augusta offers Scarlet her outstretched palms. Slowly and without losing eye contact with her Scarlet unbuttons Augusta's cuffs and then slowly unclips the front of her blouse.

Augusta instinctively reaches to her own breasts.

"Drop your hands or I will cut your fingers off," growls Scarlet.

The menace in her voice matches the threat of her words such that Augusta drops her arms to her side. Within seconds Scarlet twitches Augusta's blouse open and slides it from her shoulders leaving her bare to the room.

Again her hands twitch in an instinctive attempt to protect her modesty.

"No more warnings," hisses Scarlet. Scarlet's finger tips drift lazily over Augusta's soft flat tummy along her ribs then over her large full mounds before massaging her tiny but hardening pink nipples.

235

Scarlet smiles then slowly steps back from her.

"Stretch your arms along the beams."

Augusta, does as commanded, stretching her arms along the horizontal beam as if a slave awaiting crucifixion.

Scarlet reaches for her bull whip and in a blur of cracking leather has the tail wrapped around Augusta's palms and the beam moulding them as one.

She reaches for another bull whip and in a blink its tail has Augusta's other wrist moulded to the beam.

Scarlet pulls a knife and slices the tails from the rest of the whip, letting the handles fall loudly to the floor.

Using a taper lit by the fire, Scarlet lights five large candles and places each on the beam immediately above Augusta's head.

And then they all wait, and wait. They wait until the body of the first candle splits and the hot wax runs then drips like a river of molten lava across the beam.

The lust is initially in the anticipation for Scarlet. The arousal clear from the far away twinkle in her eyes, the slightly parted lips, the heavier slower breathing, as the river of wax nears the edge of the beam where it must drip upon Augusta.

The soft moan drifts from her into the room as the first hot drips land like hot salty come on Augusta's cheeks, her forehead, then body, rapidly turning from translucent to hardened white.

The other candles start to split and within seconds a steady waterfall of hot wax drips onto Augusta.

Each drip of the hot rain causes Augusta to gasp, twitch, flinch or growl. As much as she might try though she cannot disguise the pleasure she derives from it. That simple moment when the wax burns in its clear sexual torture then like a spent lover turns into its benign hard wax.

Scarlet and Black watch as Augusta's mind takes her aroused body into its own dark corner of depravity. Her eyes now closed, a soft serene smile breaking across her face. A smile that widens as Scarlet cuts the jodhpurs from her with her cut throat then pulls her head back hard by her long auburn hair so that the wax starts to drip directly onto her bare defenceless pussy.

"Burn my beautiful Princess, burn," Scarlet whispers into her ear. "I can smell your arousal from here whore."

"No, No," gasps Augusta.

Scarlet releases her hair, stands before her and slides the tips of her fingers to the edge of her cunt.

"So you don't want me to touch you?"

Whilst Augusta's eyes cry of depraved want, her mouth defies her,

"Don't touch me. I am your future Queen! I'll have your fucking head."

"Feisty suddenly aren't we?" smiles Scarlet.

Scarlet walks to Black and kisses him hard, letting her hand drop to his cock pressing hard against his breeches.

"Good, you're enjoying this as much as I am."

By the time Scarlet next faces Augusta she has her favourite flogger pulled tight between her hands.

"So Princess, it's my head you want...Oh dear that really doesn't give me an incentive to be kind to you now does it?"

The first time the leather tassels hit Augusta's stomach she cries out loudly. The second blow shatters the wax from her skin into the air like snow.

Scarlet is a true mistress of her dark art. The blows gradually change from their assault of Augusta's thighs and upper torso into a sustained assault of her nipples and hood.

First Augusta's skin pinks, then the swollen wheals spread across her flesh like ancient tree roots looking for moisture. Finally, tiny traces of blood prickle at the surface before smearing into small patches.

Again Augusta cannot hide her arousal.

"More."

"What did you say, whore Princess?"

"More...I want more."

"Whore."

Black watches as the punishment unfolds. Watches as Augusta's eyes full of lust and want seduce and lure Scarlet. Watches as Augusta slowly moans her pleasure to Scarlet. Almost incoherent obscenities that build into a steady rhythm that match in time the aching waves building inside her.

"You want me to touch you don't you, whore?" goads Scarlet.

"Yes."

"Then a promise?"

"What?" Augusta almost pleads breathlessly.

"Promise me that when my head is on a pike at the Tower you will kiss my lips in front of your husband. Just don't be surprised when my severed head kisses you back."

The mental image triggers the ascent to Augusta's orgasm.

"Yes promise, I promise."

"Then kiss me like it now."

And with that Scarlet kisses Augusta's soft open mouth just as her small fingers spread her hood and fuck her soaking and ripe cunt.

Scarlet can feel her own musky juices spreading onto her thighs as Augusta comes gripping her muscles tight around Scarlet's fingers.

Her long moan and whimper cry deep into Scarlet's mouth where they echo before in a staccato of gasps she looks Scarlet in the eyes and kisses her.

As their kiss breaks Augusta feels Black untying her wrists before he lifts her into his arms and carries her into the adjoining bedroom. There he lays her and starts to undress.

Augusta now consumed by her depraved lust leans on all fours towards him and urgently sucks his glistening helmet into her ready mouth.

Like a whore possessed by witchcraft she sucks hard. She then sucks at the second cock offered to her. The long hard ivory cock that protrudes from deep within Scarlet's own wet aching cunt.

Her lust is such she does not hesitate to suck at them both. It is Scarlet that breaks away and positions herself in a sitting position on the bed. Black pulls Augusta's head from his cock by her hair and now more gently steers her back into the bed until her puckered anus is resting tight against the head of Scarlet's cock.

Slowly, so slowly, the puckered anus stretches with every small probing push made by Scarlet until the cock slides through her resistance. She takes it inch by inch controlling the initial hurt with her breathing.

Black lowers her back onto Scarlet's chest and rolls his wet helmet around the rim of Augusta's tight young cunt.

Her eyes open in alarm, as Black slowly eases his cock against her,

"Shh. Just relax."

She is so wet that Black's cock slowly fills her. She can feel both cocks rubbing against each other separated only by that thin membrane within her.

And so they fuck her slowly. As Scarlet withdraws to the tip of her stretched red anus, Black buries his cock deep until his pelvic bones slap hard against her thighs.

With Scarlet taking Augusta's weight, Black lowers his head to her breasts and starts to lick at the open wounds, his mouth filling with the tell-tale taste of blood.

The stings from his saliva sends shocks through her already sensitive nerve endings. His soft wet mouth folds around the cut across her nipple. He swishes his saliva across the hardening stem before he sucks, first rhythmically like a feeding baby then hard like torture.

Augusta feels Scarlet slip her hands over her mouth from behind her and holds them tight so she can barely take in air. Scarlet fucks her arse hard and fast whilst Black leaves his cock still inside her, his mouth continuing to tease her wounds. Augusta tries to breathe and moan but she cannot, her mouth held as it is. She feels so lightheaded through the lack of oxygen that the pleasure feels ever more sensitive, ever more focused. It is only as Scarlet feels her near to faint that she releases her hands for just long enough for her to gasp in air before clamping them back over her mouth.

Augusta is lost in her pleasure. She rides the ivory cock like it is a stallion to be tamed. Her moans lost in Scarlet's hands, like a ship in the deep mist, as Black now renews his pounding of her slick wet cunt.

And then she comes. Comes so hard so deeply her juices bathe Black's cock before leaking from her in little gushes. The hands finally released so she can release her frustrated moans and gasp in air.

But he does not stop, Scarlet does not stop. Fucking her like she is mere meat they pound at her body, driving her into a sexual delirium where she babbles the words her tortured mind sends to her.

Her eyes open as she feels Black's cock twitch.

"Come, come in me, come now."

Their eyes just inches apart, lock on each other's. Hers begging him to come. His slowly drifting into hers as he feels that exquisite pain of his impending release. Their noses almost touching, their mouths sharing the same panted air.

Black cries loudly into the room as his come impregnates the future Queen. She pulls his face to hers and kisses him hard as she imagines his come as tiny golden angels flying through her veins to every tip of her body.

And then they slump, the three of them in a tangled wreckage of limbs on the bed, lost in their individual moments. Augusta stroking Black's now limp cock and Scarlet lapping lazily at the mixed come that oozes from Augusta's stretched cunt.

There are three more days of depraved pleasure before Augusta's sense of duty and Scarlet and Black's fear that the net will be closing in on them, leads them to agree that Augusta must now be released and returned to Frederick. But she makes them promise one last adventure before she leaves.

And so it is on the fourth morning after her capture that three highwaymen wait in the woods, their horses snorting steam into the autumnal air, their pistols at the ready waiting for the Prince's mail coach to come into view. And as they wait Augusta smiles affectionately at Scarlet, then slides her hand through her blouse and feels her pussy pulsate as she strokes the wounds that now paint her torso, wondering just what her darling fiancé, Prince Frederick of England will think when she bares her broken body for him.

Miss Scarlet Kiss

The first black sedan screeches to a halt on the gravel path. The driver looks on nervously as the two passengers, suit and trilby clad, and each with their own tommy gun held at the ready, leap out and head to the front door of the Crypt.

They are greeted by two similar clad and armed attendants who wave them a wary welcome. The first taps at the iron clad door and whispers that night's code through the peeled back eye view. Satisfied with the response the two gangsters head back to the gravel road and wave the second sedan in.

The second sedan pulls in more sedately. Suited men step out from either side of the rear and a third who has been seated between them steps out behind them.

He is escorted to the front door. He walks coolly and calmly in crisp uniform steps. His beauty, made or crushed by the three scars that line his right cheekbone. At a guess thirteen stone, sharp suit, starched white shirt, thin tie, black polished brogues.

The four armed men stand like a guard of honour as he enters the vestibule flanked by his escorts. He knocks three times on the waiting door. The eye view slides open and a surly pair of eyes stare back.

The peephole closes and the heavy door swings open.

From the silence of the world outside he walks into the jazz, drug and alcohol fuelled world of the Crypt.

"Welcome to the Crypt, Mr," surly eyes growls before laughing at him.

The man neither smiles nor acknowledges the doorman, but instead walks the short distance to the balcony in front of him and looks on to the hedonistic riot unravelling on the floor below.

He has heard of the Crypt – few in prohibition era Detroit haven't. The club controlled by the Grim Reaper himself, Slim "slow death," Soldatti. A place so hedonistic the Devil himself would blush.

And now, he is here he can see all that he has heard is true and more.

The music is loud, so loud it vibrates through his body. The orchestra jiggling in time to the three hot trumpets whipping the dancing couples into a frenzy.

The dancers all so beautiful. The women in sheer dresses disguising nothing of their toned bareness beneath. The men suit clad but shirtless revealing their defined pecs.

A squeal as one male dancer pulls a dress over one young dancers head and buries his mouth around her hard nipple.

The man looks over his shoulder at his escorts and slowly descends the marble steps.

His eyes take in the hedonistic beauty of all before him.

The beautiful women posing naked as the Venus de Milo with hoses shooting champagne from between their legs into the pool below where it is scooped up in punch glasses in ever increasing quantities.

The young men and women covered in their entirety in chocolate bought out naked on silver serving platters. Each one placed on a small altar where they are devoured by 100 different tongues till they are cleaned and sexually spent.

The skimpily clad tightrope walkers breathing dragon size flames walking high overhead.

The naked women serving as roulette tables, the wheels sitting on their stomachs as people bet their chips on the black and red squares painted onto their bodies.

He walks through the crowd. The same uniform footsteps. No acknowledgement from those around him. He only stops once as a man, much too worse for wear stumbles and falls in front of him. The fallen man fumbles to his feet, mumbles apologies and scampers so as to disappear into the gathered throng.

No one makes eye contact with the man. No one greets him. No one touches him. No one reaches for his hand. Especially his hands. They cannot risk the consequence.

No, whilst they are all there in part because of him, they will not acknowledge him because within the hour he will be dead. Dead like the others with his broken body and face found floating in the river or buried in a shallow grave in the woods.

Because tonight he will be fighting to the death. A bare knuckle contest till he or his opponent is dead. His opponent who has now fought and killed six men. For the first time since he was a child he knows what it is to feel fear.

His name is Black and he has signed up to this willingly. The Detroit force so corrupt the President has secretly sent in a special team from the FBI to solve the mystery of the six brutally murdered men and the gang racket they believe is behind it.

The plan had worked well so far. They had quickly identified that each of the victims had been picked from the jobless queues, no doubt tempted by a pay day beyond their wildest dreams.

Black had easily caught the eye of Soldatti's chief recruitment officer as he had picked a fight with the brute of a guy next to him and laid him out cold.

The purse is good. Win and you get $500 and Scarlet, Soldatti's favourite show girl. Lose and die.

Right now, as he stares through the crowds and sees not one friendly face, as he looks at the smirking face of Soldatti as his girls take tens of thousands of dollars in bets, he prays for a speedy and painless death.

The orchestra strikes up a belting finale. The young couples now in various stages of undress gyrate themselves to dance heaven.

Black recognises many faces from the pictures of movie magazines and the family portraits of influential politicians. He really is in as deep as it gets.

The song reaches its dizzying climax and many of the dancers with it. As their bodies heave back into the conscious and their breathing finally slows, they pick up their discarded clothing and pour like eels through cracks back to their tables.

"Ladies, gentleman, distinguished guests, please take your seats. Normally our next act would be the star of the show but tonight I know there is something you are all dying (a ripple of laughter), I say dying (a louder ripple) to see so without further ado let me introduce the Queen of the Crypt, Miss Scarlet Kiss."

The compere leaves the stage and the lights dim until bar the pin pricks of cigarette ends and the occasional flickering of lighters the entire club is in darkness.

Black senses the opportunity to run, but is drawn to stay and watch as the slow bass line starts its simple chords.

Some people say they can remember the moment war was declared or a famous Politician or Actor died. Anyone who has been to the Crypt remembers the first time they saw Miss Scarlet Kiss. Black was no different.

The lights above slowly illuminate the stage below and then she enters. Oozing a heady mix of foreplay and tortured soul, her hips sway like a tree in a gentle breeze. Her long legs glide free from the passive restraint of her black cocktail dress. Her eyes, so blue, like aquamarine piercing into the audience before her. Her lips so soft but also capable of signing the death warrant of anyone who should try to kiss them.

"We love you, Scarlet," comes one call from the audience. Others near him hiss at him to quieten.

And then she starts, her breath coating the microphone like warm honey before her soft deep voice tells the tale of a broken love, a broken man, a broken heart.

As she starts the penultimate verse, the audience break into spontaneous applause. The small area on which Scarlet stands rises like a black marbled altar, four feet above the ground.

Thousands of tiny golden stars, rings and glitter flakes flutter from the ceiling slowly absorbing Scarlet in their midst.

As the song ends, the audience stand and clap and cheer their appreciation.

Scarlet becoming ever more obscured from them unzips the back of her dress, slides the material teasingly over her shoulder and just as she becomes entirely invisible to the audience, lets the dress slip to the floor leaving her entirely bare.

The already subdued light, dims still further as the golden snow continues to fall in silence like poppies on Armistice Day.

For a whole two minutes the club is silent. No one reaches for their glass, no one lights a cigarette, no one as much as whispers.

Slowly the lights around the altar start to glow and it looks to all there that Scarlet has disappeared through the floor. But suddenly and softly, the surface of the altar starts to move like a gentle swaying mass. A loud animalistic roar fills the hall and with a swish of a tail and a flick of her own beautiful long blond hair, the audience see Scarlet laying with two live jewel encrusted leopards, one forming a pillow, the other at her feet, its soft paws wrapped over her thighs.

The leopard at her feet stands to face the audience and roars not once but twice marking its territory before slowly nuzzling its head between Scarlet's calves until she opens her legs wide.

The leopard like the most tender of lovers slowly uses its long pink tongue to tease the inside of her thighs. Scarlett leans back into the soft fur of the leopard on which she lays now gradually pulling at its ear and the soft fur on its head, as her eyes close.

The tongue now lapping at her pussy lips, surprisingly tender but so large it can tease both her clit and cunt at the same time. The leopard feeding freely on the juices flowing from her.

Scarlet feeling those waves slowly building within her. Feeling for the supporting leopard's tail and whipping its coarse tip against her bare exposed breasts, bringing out small pink wheals criss- crossing her skin.

"I want her," says Black,

"Son, she is Soldatti's girl, he'd rather kill you both first."

No one can take their eyes from Scarlet. Sharing with her that long slow tongue and cruel live whip. Her breathing quickens, her hips start to thrust and seconds later her long cry of pleasure fills the silent club as her orgasm drives uncontrollably through her body, making her ankles rise and hold tight around the leopard's back.

With that the club falls into complete darkness and the audience explode into a crescendo of appreciation.

"Even you dying isn't going to match that, son."

Black found he really couldn't argue with his escort's summary.

His escort tells Black that the next time the lights come on he is to follow them onto the dance floor where the fight will take place.

Dutifully he follows and strips himself slowly of all but his breeches preferring to fight bare foot once he realises how slippery the floor might be.

His welcome from the audience is muted bar the odd wolf whistle from some drunken girls.

The same could not be said of his opponent. The calls of "Beast, Beast, Beast," starting as a rumbling but building to a foot-stamping chant as the nineteen stone monster moves onto the floor.

The beast, a former contender for the boxing heavyweight championship but now a paid killer for Soldatti. Waving to his audience and giving a thumbs up like the champion gladiator to Caesar.

The compere introduces the two fighters to the crowd. Scarlet is to wish them both luck.

"Kill him, I want out," She whispers in Black's ear.

The fight is long and bloody. Black's speed pays early dividends as he catches the Beast with some early blows to the head, but soon as if tired of a fly buzzing around his head the Beast charges Black scooping him onto the floor and kicking him in the ribs. All would have been lost if the Beast had not played to the audience as he made to stamp on Black's head giving him the opportunity to roll away.

For the next fifteen minutes the fight takes a similar course. Black sapping the Beasts stamina, with fast telling punches that cut his opponents face at will, but then the Beast's strength overpowering Black and punching him inside till he can feel ribs crack and organs bruise.

But then the vital mistake. One shot to his ear leaves the Beast deafened and in his terrible rage he picks up a wine bottle from a table, cracks it then charges Black.

Black avoids the flashing blow twice before catching a stinging swipe across his chest. Nearly exhausted they stand barely one foot apart before with his last ounce of speed Black pokes his fingers into Beasts eyes and rams his own hand still holding the broken bottle into his throat.

There is silence as the Beast slumps to the floor and the lights are killed.

"I want my prize, Soldatti," cries Black in the darkness "I want Scarlet."

The lights come on just as three of Soldatti's men aim at Black with their guns. The audience howl their displeasure.

"He's won fair and square Soldatti," cries one,

"Give him the Prize," shouts another

"Give him Scarlet."

Despite the bile and anger rising within him, Soldatti is aware that the club is turning against him, aware that with all the famous people present the influence he has taken so long to build with be lost.

"Friends, friends," he calls using his arms to usher calm. "Of course he must have Scarlet."

Soldatti sits pensively whispering to his henchmen as the music strikes up to announce Scarlet's arrival.

She is standing tall on the altar in her black silk robe and black stockinged feet. She slides the robe to the floor leaving her in matching bra and girdle. Slowly she releases each stocking from its clip to the girdle and lowers it along her leg to her ankle where like a hungry bird pecking at a worm she takes it from her toe. Throwing it theatrically high into the air, the audience follow its looping path in the air to its soft landing at her feet.

Her hands behind her back, unclipping her bra. Holding the cups till she allows them to fall from her grasp releasing her full firm breasts and light hard nipples. The club is silent again entranced with this woman. Her fingers hooked into the now unzipped girdle she teases it over her Amazonian hips then strong thighs till it loses traction and joins her stockings on the floor.

She looks to Black and invites him with a slow curved beckoning finger. With pain still racking his ribs Black shuffles towards her, his torso covered in scratches, wheals and bruises. His right eye, cheekbone and lip slightly bloodied.

"Kiss me," she says in that voice.

"I am bloodied," says Black protectively.

"Shhhh kiss me," she says one finger pressed tight to her lips.

Scarlet gently pulls Black's slightly lowered head back by his hair, wipes the drying blood from the side of his mouth with her thumb and lets her soft partly opened mouth touch his. The honeyed breath and small darting tongue overwhelm Black's exhausted senses and he almost collapses with the desire and pleasure she brings. Another kiss, longer, even softer.

From the corner of her eye Scarlet sees Soldatti in an ever increasing state of agitation. She whispers gently in Black's ear,

"You are a brave man. I want out. We must provoke him, Soldatti, do whatever it takes."

Scarlet lays back on the cushions spread on the altar and opens her legs to receive Black. He slides his trousers to the floor, revealing his tight toned dimpled arse cheeks and semi stiff shaft. Sinking to his knees, he reaches for one stocking and ties Scarlet's wrists above her head. She groans and his mouth kisses, sucks and bites her chin, neck and shoulders before his soft tongue traces a line around her nipples.

His mouth then tracing a path from her tummy to her thighs then back to her bare defenceless pussy lips.

His tongue glides gently on the outer skin of her pussy lips making no effort to break through them. The tingles make Scarlet moan slightly and grab at the cushions above her head.

His tongue finally breaks through her hood and is coated with her free flowing nectar teasing his taste buds, seducing him to drink from her. Slowly just the very tip of his tongue glides to her hard clit. A tiny hard bud. Hard like a ruby. The tip of the tongue touches it as light as air itself massaging the bud in small circles. The rhythm and pressure build and with it Scarlet's moan which now starts to echo through the club. She is no longer in Soldatti's world but her own where her man can pleasure her. She pinches at her own nipples, a deep hard unforgiving pinch complementing the shuddering tingles that now flow through her pussy. She involuntarily thrusts her hips onto Black's tongue controlling the pressure he gives and then she cries – cries like a soul released from torture as the orgasm runs through her sending flames of fire through her tummy and thighs.

Her eyes barely focus before she feels herself being gently turned and raised onto all fours. Her wrists still bound her ankles are now tied. His still strong fingers spread her bottom cheeks and his tongue soon gently kisses then flicks at the delicious nerve endings of her anus.

His tongue gently pressing and probing her, slowly lowering the guarding muscles until his tongue breaks their resistance. Her gasp leaves mouths agape in the audience.

Now content she is sufficiently pleasured and lubricated Black kneels behind her and places the swollen head of his cock against her anus. Slowly from their subtle combined pressure his cock enters her inch by inch. He allows her time to let the initial pain settle into that deep throbbing ache before he starts to fuck her. Fuck her with long slow strokes, nearly sliding from her then filling her with the full length of his shaft.

She grips the cushions ever tighter, her mouth gripping at the material. The audience start to clap in rhythm to Black's strokes. Just a few at first, then more, and more until the synchronised clap fills the club like thunder.

Soldatti is incandescent with rage. His face flushed red, his fists clenched. She has never let him use her this way.

The rhythm quickens as does the clapping. They all hear her murmur

"Come inside me baby, please."

The golden snow again starts to fall from the ceiling quickly covering Scarlet and Black, like golden Gods from ancient Rome.

The rhythm quickens still further. Black's tight balls now slapping hard against Scarlet's pussy lips as his shaft fills her.

She knows he is close to his orgasm. She murmurs her own thoughts out loud,

"Fuck me, fuck me, fill me, fill me with your hot come."

She hears Black's long animalistic groan roar like the leopards around the club as he twitches and his come erupts deep inside her.

They slump in a single indistinguishable clump of arms and legs, their still forms soon completely covered in gold.

Above the roar of the crowd, there is a single gunshot. A shot from Soldatti's pistol as he breaks free from those at his table who are trying to stop him exacting his ruthless despatch of Black and Scarlet.

Soldatti stumbles across the floor, pistol at the ready, clearly deranged beyond all reason.

The audience start to clear the club in a mass blind panic as he approaches the altar.

The layer of gold starts to shift as before. One last cruel smile from Soldatti as he aims his pistol. The smile turns to one of horror and unmatched fear as the two leopards leap from their golden blanket on the altar. One leaps instinctively for the gun holding arm and the other for his throat.

Soldatti is no more.

In the small room beneath the stage, the room they have just switched with the leopards Scarlet and Black catch their breath, briefly giggling like children before holding each other tight.

They have heard Soldatti's scream of death then gunfire as the FBI agents pile in as the audience flees.

They later hear the battle was brief but bloody. Soldatti's gang are dead or captured.

They head to the changing rooms. Black finds some overalls then watches Scarlet dress, knowing inside that nothing will ever quite be the same again.

Malevolence

The annals of the underworld in London have well chronicled the tales of the Krays to the East and the Richardson's to the South. With stories of the infamous night at the Blind Beggar to the unusual dentistry methods used by Mad Frankie Fraser in the grease filled car repair garages in the darkest parts of South London.

History has however been less kind to Tony Staines. Staines the psychotic leader of the Staines gang in West London in the mid-1960s. The undoubted master of every protection racket nightclub, pub and casino to the west of Westminster.

Untroubled by his rivals, with whom he enjoyed an uneasy pact. A pact based almost entirely upon geography and their respective resources rather than affection or affinity.

Although the Krays had much of Soho in their pockets, there was one street there controlled by Staines.

Rupert Street. One of the more risqué parts of town where anything went. Where even gay or bisexual guys could find a home behind a thick velvet curtain and dark lit booths. A very selective clientele with heavy purses in these days when homosexuality remained illegal in its most basic sexual form.

Stories were rife of Staines's huge sexual appetite with its distinctly violent edge. Of his appetite for men and women especially the younger, prettier of each kind.

It was never a surprise to see Staines with one of the beautiful croupiers on one arm and sometimes a pretty young guy on the other leaving his flagship casino, the Pink Flamingo through its back door for his private flat at 25a Rupert Street where she or they would be expected to meet his varied and dangerous demands.

He had not used his favourite girl Scarlet for the last three weeks. He had used her a little too roughly last time. He had no fear at all of killing but had not intended the harm he had caused her as her rib had pierced her lung under the weight of his punishment leaving her gasping like a fish on the floor of the bedroom.

He had paid well for the silence of the Doctors that night. Whilst he delighted in Scarlet's beauty and own unusual tastes his desire to save her arose not just from a wish to preserve her for his use but more a wish to avoid investigation by those Police controlled by the Krays rather than he.

But he knew that tonight she would be back at her usual place at the roulette wheel. Winning the punters confidence with her gentle soft chatter and twinkling silver green eyes.

He really would have left her alone if he had not arrived. Sir Charles Wilderton a promising back bench MP destined for bigger things in Parliament.

Sir Charles, the pretty young man to whom gossip was no stranger.

Sir Charles was immediately seduced by the free gaming chips and the chilled complimentary champagne bought to him by the beautiful Scarlet.

Even when his lack of gambling skills should have seen him stripped of all he owned he had miraculously won. Won just enough for him to whoop slightly too loudly before he found himself hugging Scarlet who winced under her corset from her still healing wound.

He delighted in her soft seductive chat, her flirtatious giggle. Still the free champagne flowed. Scarlet barely flinched as Sir Charles's hand had for too long held her dressed breast. Had for too long nuzzled gently at her ear promising her ever more valuable riches were she to sleep with him.

Scarlet's shift was due to finish at eleven. She smelled trouble as the word came down to her at 10.50 that Staines required her to stay until two.

Just before midnight Staines had introduced himself to Sir Charles as the owner of the Casino, unleashing upon Staines his perfect smile and the jewellery that adorned his fingers like the window display at a jewellers in Hatton Garden. Sir Charles was far too inebriated to notice Scarlet flinch as Staines's hand had drifted across her shoulders.

Staines had left shortly after but had reappeared 15 minutes or so later with a flurry of more champagne and canapes to ensure that Sir Charles needs were being met.

Sir Charles now the worse for wear and entirely smitten with Scarlet virtually hugs Staines as he asks him all too loudly just what he would have to do to have Scarlet for the night. Scarlet had hoped Staines would deter him but their collusional laugh did little to allay her fears.

Scarlet thought her shift had finally finished when Sir Charles had failed to return promptly from the gents and she had hurried to her coat in the cloakroom

"Sorry, honey," said Dolores the attendant. "You are wanted at 25a."

Scarlet's heart sank. The ache in her ribs and her lungs, still yet to reach capacity, reminded her all too well what was expected of her there.

"No, please, Dolores, can't you tell Mr Staines you couldn't find me?"

"We both know I can't do that, Scarlet."

Dolores noticed Scarlet stroke her side then bite her lip.

"Take care, darling, eh."

Scarlet smiled what they both knew was an artificial reassurance before she changed back into her skirt and thin jumper and headed for the back door which would take her to the door at 25a.

She knew she would be used, hurt and violated. She knew the signs. Sir Charles needed to be impressed at whatever cost. Staines' bodyguards had been sent to the all night café instead of guarding the front door. The sound of hot trumpet poured into the street from the open window like steam. She could hear the clinks of glasses from the pavement below.

She hesitated slightly before pressing the buzzer and shuddered slightly as his voice answered.

"Ah, Scarlet. I'm so glad you could join us. I have left you a change of clothes in the dressing room. Please join Sir Charles and I upstairs when you are ready."

The front door was released and she stepped through into the dimly lit hall then into the dressing room to the left.

She was used to having to dress or undress for Staines. He had a Roman fixation and she was sure he thought of himself as a modern day Caesar. But instead of the toga or some such, the outfit that awaited her was the costume of a nun.

Now Scarlet was not particularly religious, but nor did she have any wish to affront the God she did believe in, especially if as usual Staines wanted photos. These were religious times and she shivered at the consequences of disrespecting those that she still feared within herself.

She knew however that right there and then she was more fearful of Staines than she was of her God and after promising to him under her breath that she would make her peace with him another time, she changed into the costume

She struggled up the stairs under the length of the cassock, then knocked at the door to the lounge and awaited his command.

"Come in, Scarlet."

She entered, only her beautiful face on view under the habit. Staines, jacket removed, shirt sleeves rolled up and gun holster tucked under his arm pit pours her a glass of champagne.

"A drink, Sister?"

Sir Charles lets out an alcohol fuelled titter.

"Thank you."

Scarlet sips at the bubbles hoping for a quick hit to numb her a little from what is to come.

She watches Staines close the window and pull the curtains. She smiles to herself as the flashing cartoon images of Staines strip club opposite reflect from the curtain onto Sir Charles and the wall behind him.

"I have promised you to Sir Charles for the night, Scarlet. Don't let me have cause to be disappointed will you?"

The words said so matter of fact yet carrying a menace capable of her demise. Scarlet downs the champagne and holds it to Staines for a refill.

As she gulps at the refilled glass she feels that familiar turmoil. The turmoil that whilst the life she has repulses her it is the only one that can satisfy her needs, her dark craving. The only way her wants can be satiated. That violation. The hate she feels for herself tempered by the desire for that release.

It is Staines who now standing behind Scarlet lowers the skirt of the cassock to her ankles. Still a nun from the waist up she is bare bar stockings and heels from the waist down.

Her eyes are locked with Sir Charles. He cannot resist but let his eyes fall first to her feet and slim ankles, then her long, slim, stockinged legs then her tight hood on full view below the tightly trimmed hair. Scarlet can smell his lust. Her excitement feeds on it.

"I would suggest you should be on the bed old boy," Staines gently mocks.

Although Sir Charles smiles in return, Scarlet senses the menace just as she has in her lovers many times before.

She watches as Sir Charles rises from his chair, slides off his polished brogues and socks, then lowers and kicks off his trousers then damp ridden and bulging pants.

The whore within her wants this cock. This surprisingly long curved, thin, hard shaft with its silken wet purple helmet.

Sir Charles lays on his back across the day bed and waits for this beautiful corrupt, broken Nun to suck him.

Scarlet lowers herself to her knees before him.

"Are you not planning on praying for forgiveness Sister, for your slutty ways?"

She hears Sir Charles moan gently and lets it soak into her mind that the corruption of this child of God is his tormented fantasy.

Scarlet places her palms in prayer and closes her eyes.

"Forgive me father for what I am about to do. Forgive me for being a whore and for wanting this man's dirty cock to defile me, to come inside me, to break me. Amen."

Her voice so soft, so innocent. She hears a long slow groan escape Sir Charles wet lips. She could have lied to herself that her prayer was designed to make Sir Charles come more quickly, to speed the end of this torment but to herself she cannot lie.

She is for now this Nun and now she wants to be defiled.

And so her mouth closes around that swollen and salty helmet, her beautiful eyes imploring humanity from Sir Charles. Her tongue rolling around his sensitive underside before it slowly fills and fucks his come hole.

His head rolls back and slowly he thrusts his hips, delighting as Scarlet grips his shaft tight so she can control the inches her soft wet mouth can take.

The next feeling is one she has felt only once before. It is Staines who pulls her by her hair through her habit from his cock and places the noose over her head.

As her mouth returns to its torture of Sir Charles shaft she already knows that Staines will be looping the rope through the hoop in the ceiling and handing the other end into Sir Charles care.

He cannot resist the first tug that makes her gasp for air.

It is one of the few confessions she has made to Staines. The one that the noose above all else turns her on. The bastard.

The noose is pulled tighter and Scarlet is forced to follow until she is straddling Sir Charles. Staines is watching from his chair, nursing his drink. She knows those eyes. The ones that shout of arousal. His own lust building such that she knows he will shortly erupt if not sexually spent.

She holds her cunt tight against this aching helmet and slowly, slowly forces herself onto it until she swallows it inside of her.

"God she is fucking wet, whore," mocks Sir Charles, and it's true she is.

And she wants this. She wants him pumping his cock deep inside her like he is now. Changing the depth that he enters her, changing the angle.

She senses rather than sees Staines rise from his chair and move behind her. She doesn't see him suck on his finger before he presses it against her anus, then slowly ease it inside. Scarlet cannot suppress her moan.

The finger is but a tool to ease the passage of something else. She has not seen Staines take the shot pourer from the drinks' cabinet and insert it into the half full champagne bottle. But she does now hear Staines suck on it to lubricate it before it is gently eased into her behind.

She feels Staines shake the bottle and then the rush of cold liquid flow into her as the bubbles and alcohol pop and tease her very core.

"Enjoy it Scarlet, its Moet."

Scarlet is getting slowly lost in her own depravity. As she rises to the tip of Sir Charles cock she breathes, but as she forces her way down so deep she feels him bruise her very inside, the noose pulls tight cutting off her air and another rush of wet teasing bubbles surge through her.

She no longer recognises herself as herself, a Nun or even a person. She is simply a vessel through which pleasure travels.

With every tug of the rough rope and every gasp she lets out, with every rush of the bubbles inside her and every deep bruising thrust, she nears her climax.

And as she cries, and she babbles, she hears herself praying, though to whom or for what she doesn't know. But deep in her self-conscious she knows it turns Sir Charles on more and more such that his thrusts get deeper, faster and more desperate.

She comes deep over his cock, feeling her pussy muscles spasm around his shaft. Her come pours through her cunt until she is sure in her head that it must coat his balls.

Somewhere deep and far away she hears his moans, feels his twitch and she knows she must get off him or be pregnant.

Jerking the rope from his control she rises and sinks to his knees before him just in time for his hot salty come to fill her mouth.

The sound of her heart beat fills the room. The only sound louder are the moans of Sir Charles as he twitches in his aftershocks.

"Oh, Scarlet."

The menacing request drips through her mind until it lands like heavy rain on her brain.

Slowly her blurred vision clears and her breathing slows. Staines is in his chair stroking his bare, hard cock.

She slinks to the floor like a cat and crawls until she is on all fours before him. She swallows on him hard, but knows she is but the aperitif. She knows that look. The look that tells her it is Sir Charles who must pleasure Staines. Must pleasure him not only for his sexual satisfaction but also to ensure that Sir Charles is his bitch and is in his control for evermore.

Slowly with her senses returning she knows what she has to do. She smiles at Staines and then slowly pulling herself up heads to Sir Charles. Kissing him softly on the mouth she pulls him gently by the hair and leads him like a dog on a lead before lowering him to his knees before Staines's erect cock.

She forces his head over Staines's swollen shaft and forces it down. There is no resistance, there is no hesitation. In his search for pleasure Sir Charles mouth folds around Staines's hard cock and sucks furiously.

Scarlet seeks out the noose and pulls the rope down from its loop. She slowly ties the wrists of Sir Charles and Staines around one arm of the chair then tangles the rope around the neck of Sir Charles before restraining their other wrists around the other arm.

Still Sir Charles with his virgin mouth works the length of Staines's cock.

The jazz record finally comes to an end and Scarlet drifts towards the player and restarts the tunes slowly increasing the volume.

"Hey not so loud," she teases as Staines starts to growl.

Scarlet pulls Sir Charles's head back by the hair and kisses him hard and then Staines. Her tongue dancing with each wanting mouth.

She pulls the gun from Staines holster and points it slowly at Sir Charles's temples.

"Suck harder, suck harder, whore."

Staines looks at Scarlet and starts to laugh.

"Yes suck harder, whore." Staines mocks before he turns his head to Scarlet.

"You know I love you right, but I can never let you live after this."

"I know," murmurs Scarlet.

And in a way she means it. In a way she has known this is the fate that the night intended.

Sir Charles continues to suck hard. His saliva dribbling along Staines's cock.

"Suck, fucker," shouts Scarlet.

And Sir Charles does, drawing ever louder moans from Staines's open mouth.

"Tony, you're too loud, way too loud."

Scarlet reaches for Sir Charles pants, sniffs them provocatively, then stuffs them deep into Staines mouth.

"That's better now fuck his mouth."

Scarlet thrusts Sir Charles mouth hard, up and down Staines's Cock. She hears them both growl their respective pleasures.

"Are you ready to come?" asks Scarlet "Are you ready to come?"

Staines now lost in his moment thrusts his cock ever deeper inside Sir Charles's mouth.

And still Scarlet waves Staines's gun at Sir Charles's temples.

"Suck, suck harder."

Scarlet looks at Staines and Staines returns the look, his eyes smiling from behind the taste of the pants filling his mouth.

And she waits and she waits. And then she smiles and strokes Staines hair until he comes deep into Sir Charles's mouth.

It is at this moment that she pulls the trigger and sends the bullet hurtling through Sir Charles defenceless skull. Sir Charles's face has an expression of surprise just before he dies. He slumps face down, his mouth still folded around Staines now soft wet cock.

Staines starts to struggle as he feels the warm wet blood seep through from Sir Charles into his white shirt.

Scarlett coolly empties the barrel of the gun until it is empty of bullets then strokes each chamber and the handle with her cassock cleaning it of her prints.

She smiles then slides it into Staines restrained hand.

Staines fights and struggles but as much as he might try he cannot break free. He slumps back into the seat his body coated in sweat, his soft wet cock resting by Sir Charles's spunk filled mouth. And Scarlet smiles.

She pours herself a drink and lights a cigarette and watches. Watches as slowly minute by minute, Staines' insanity reveals itself, layer by layer. She watches as the bright light of the reflection from the exotic dancers fills the room.

When the cigarette stops its excited glow at its butt, Scarlet drains her drink and smiles once more at Staines.

"Bye bye, Tony, it was sometimes nice knowing you."

And with that she takes her glass and heads to the dressing room where she takes off the Nun uniform and dresses.

There are still no bodyguards. The throng of the crowd milling along Rupert Street are a welcome sight.

Scarlet heads to the phone box and dials 999.

"Police please, there are gun shots. I think someone has been shot. 25a Rupert Street…"

Scarlet replaces the receiver knowing that the mere mention of this address will draw a rapid response. Indeed, she waits no more than one minute before three police cars, sirens blaring, pull up outside.

She sees Staines's bodyguards appear through the café door then slink into the crowd knowing they are too late to help.

Scarlet lights a cigarette then waits until the yellow glow of the black cab comes into view.

"Taxi, taxi," she calls.

9 781786 125996

An environmentally friendly book printed and bound in England by www.printondemand-worldwide.com

Reprint of # - C0 - 198/129/18 - PB - Lamination Gloss - Printed on 04-May-16 10:39